The woman opened the door, and took a step into the room. Mund followed and stood next to her. It was a fairly large room, filled with sewing machines, looms, and tables with balls of yarn piled on top of them. About twenty old women sat scattered around the room. Most of them were knitting, but they stopped when they saw Mund walk in.

They're scared, he thought to himself. His eyes searched their faces. Margaret's was not one of them.

"Okay, where is she?"

He heard the door slam behind him and turned to see the woman he had followed lock it from the inside. He saw her move toward the open window and he tried to stop her, but just as he reached her, the woman threw the key out the window.

The woman turned slowly around to face him. "If it's Mrs. Binton you're looking for, she left a moment ago." She smiled innocently....

He stopped and turned to look around him. Each woman held a long, gleaming knitting needle. They were all pointed at him.

# THE
# RAG BAG
# CLAN

Richard Barth

FAWCETT CREST • NEW YORK

A Fawcett Crest Book
Published by Ballantine Books
Copyright ©1978 by Richard Barth

ISBN 0-449-21814-7

Manufactured in the United States of America

First Ballantine Books Edition: February 1990

*To Ilene*

# One

SERGEANT SCHAEFFER GLANCED DOWN at the body in front of him. It must have been a professional hit. "The door wasn't forced," he said, turning to Jacobson. "Looks like she knew her murderer."

"What time did you find her?" Jacobson asked the superintendent.

"About an hour ago. I called up right away."

"Did you hear anything?"

The man shook his head. "Just came up to fix Mrs. Feiner's window. She complained it was leaking last week when we had that rain. I found her just like that—the kettle was still on.

Schaeffer looked around the tiny apartment and shook his head. "What about the money?" He held out his hand and showed the roll of bills to the superintendent. "Did you know she had it?"

The man's eyes widened. "No, officer. No idea. She was just one of them bag ladies. Never made any trouble."

"No friends?"

"Maybe over at the center . . . but none that came around here."

"Jacobson," Schaeffer said. "Morley will want us to run it down. Why don't you check on the street, then over at that center. I'll wait here till the ambulance comes."

1

Jacobson nodded, took one final look at the woman on the floor and left.

Margaret Binton did volunteer work three afternoons a week at the Flora K. Bliss Center on Ninety-eighth Street and Broadway. It was one of a few private shelters that supplied hot meals, first aid, recreation, and a limited number of beds to anyone who was in need. The center was always full of people watching quiz shows on an old Dumont TV, playing cards at the various tables in the reception room, chatting steadily in the cafeteria.

Margaret was in charge of coffee and snacks, and along with the food and drinks, she gave out cheerful greetings to the faces she recognized. She worried a lot about the women who came there, especially the quiet loners, the ones who clung to their shopping bags even when they went to get coffee. Women like Sarah Feiner and Rose Gaffery.

A handful of them stopped by in the afternoons and Margaret always carried coffee to the tables for them. If she wasn't too busy, she'd sit and talk for a few minutes before going back to the counter. She tried to pierce through their outer shells, but it rarely worked. They were always shy and guarded and Margaret continued to feel alien to their experiences and style of living. She just couldn't understand how anyone could spend their nights in doorways, abandoned buildings, or coldwater flats.

She usually found it easier to talk with Rose than with the others, and now, as she stood behind the counter pouring coffee for Rose, Margaret looked forward to the few minutes they would spend together.

While Rose was waiting for Margaret to put in the two spoons of sugar, Jacobson came up to Margaret and introduced himself.

"I was told you know Sarah Feiner?"

"Sarah? Why, of course. Sarah comes in several afternoons a week," Margaret said. "Why? What would you like to know about her?"

"All I can find out," Jacobson said. "We just found her this morning in her room. She'd been shot."

"Oh, my God . . ."

"It wasn't a robbery," Jacobson said. "When we searched the apartment we found a thousand dollars stuffed into the toe of one of her shoes. These crazy scavengers don't come across that kind of money. Maybe you know something that might give us a lead?"

Margaret shook her head. "She kept mostly to herself. Most of these ladies do." Margaret looked around for Rose but she was nowhere in sight. It wasn't like her to disappear like that, just as she was about to have coffee.

"Anything else?" Jacobson waited, but Margaret just shook her head.

"Well, if anything comes up give me a call at the Eighty-first Precinct." Margaret nodded. Jacobson looked down at the coffee Margaret was holding. "You mind?"

"No, no. Go ahead."

He picked up the styrofoam cup. "What a life!" he said, sizing up the room.

"I'm sorry," he said. "We see them all . . . thanks for the coffee." He smiled at her, tossed his cup into a trash bin, and left.

Margaret went to look for Rose in the recreation room but it was empty. Unlike her, Margaret thought, returning to her spot by the coffee machine. The rest of the day she thought about Sarah. Who would want to kill that poor old woman?

Two days later Margaret saw Rose again. Margaret was sitting on her favorite bench at Eightieth Street and Broadway. She and her friends, the old, retired people from the neighborhood, were gossiping about local headlines, feeding the pigeons handfuls of stale bread, and watching the traffic buzz around their little island. She spotted Rose across the street, sitting on a bench by herself, her bags strewn around her. Rose was dressed in the same stained clothes she had worn on Friday, and her gray hair flew around in the light breeze. Margaret got up and went over, and as Margaret approached, Rose reached down into one of the bags and pulled out a half-smoked cigarette. She didn't look over as Margaret sat down but reached into another bag and fumbled around.

"Wanna cigarette?" Rose said.

"Thanks," Margaret said, surprised at the greeting. Rose held out two half-smoked cigarettes, one a bit longer than the other. She studied them for an instant, then handed Margaret the longer one. There was a fleck of lipstick on the rim.

"You probably used to fresh 'uns. Them's the best I got."

Margaret hesitated briefly, then wiped the filter and waited for Rose to light it. The first drag was awful, but after the third puff it became a regular cigarette, one of the twenty or so Margaret smoked every day.

"Why did you leave so quickly last Friday?" Margaret asked after they had sat for a minute. "Something that policeman said . . . about Sarah?"

"Sarah?"

"Didn't you hear? She's been killed."

Rose took another puff, gently crushed the cigarette out, then carefully placed it back in the bag. When she straightened up she leaned closer to Margaret.

"If I tell you a secret now you won't be mad at me? Margaret, you gotta promise not to be mad."

"Of course not, Rose."

Rose looked around suspiciously before she spoke. "It's the money," she said, almost at a whisper.

"Money? What money?" Margaret said cautiously.

"In the trash. Over a thousand. Found it in a shirt—nice shirt. Here. I still got it." She pulled out a man's blue-plaid cotton short-sleeve shirt. It looked new.

Margaret slowly turned it over in her hands. "When did you find this?"

"'Bout a week ago, down at the bottom of one of them cans near here."

"And the money?"

"Oh, I still got it." She grinned. "Somewhere safe."

Margaret leaned back. "But what has all this got to do with Sarah?"

"Ain't it plain? Last week I seen her at the center. You wasn't around, an' she's wearing the same shirt to this one." Rose dropped her voice. "An' she was as nervous as a coot."

"Did you speak to her?"

"No. Just passing by I noticed. Also outta the pocket of her dress is stickin' a fifty. Thought that was pretty strange."

"But you should tell the police." Margaret puffed on her cigarette. "Go right now and explain about the money and everything."

Rose shook her head slowly. "No, I . . . first money I ever found an' I'm keepin' it. Don't wanta go lookin' for trouble with the cops neither. Always coming at me, nosy-bodyin' about." She stood up quickly and gathered her bags around her. "Gotta go. It's gettin' late. Sorry about Sarah."

She turned, and before Margaret could say anything she was on her way across the street, her bags strung around her like so many bumpers on a tug boat.

Margaret Binton was usually very good at keeping secrets, but Rose's remained secure only until Monday noon when Margaret walked into Eighty-first Precinct and asked for Sergeant Jacobson. She felt it was her duty.

She found Jacobson sitting at his desk in a large room. She hadn't noticed before how young and good-looking he was. A man who looked like a Bowery bum was slumped in a chair across from the desk, his feet propped on the telephone. He had a full beard, a torn jacket, and dirty trousers with rips at the cuffs. Even his fingernails were caked with dirt.

"Oh, excuse me," she said. "I'll wait."

Jacobson smiled and motioned her to another seat.

"The lady from the Bliss Center, right?"

"Yes, Margaret Binton." She glanced curiously at the other man.

"I'm Sergeant Schaeffer," the man said. "Don't mind me, I'm his alter ego."

She still looked puzzled.

"His partner. I'm a cop."

"Oh," she chuckled. "You had me fooled."

Jacobson interrupted. "What's on your mind?"

Margaret repeated Rose's story. "It may not mean anything," she concluded, "but I thought you'd like to know."

Jacobson looked over at Schaeffer, who was studying Margaret closely.

"What's this Rose Gaffery like?" he said finally. "Do you think she could be mixed up in anything?"

Margaret chuckled. "Rose? Never. She's a scavenger. All she does all day is look through garbage cans."

Jacobson leaned back. "So was Sarah Feiner."

Margaret nodded. "Oh, yes. That's right."

Schaeffer stood up and walked a few steps away, thinking, then turned around and walked back. "When did she say she found it?"

"A week ago."

"And Feiner is killed right afterward." He sat down. "There's a connection there. Maybe Gaffery's money was supposed to have been picked up by Feiner, and whoever was supposed to receive it knocked off Feiner when she couldn't produce it."

"But that means Sarah was mixed up in something," Margaret protested.

"Running payments of some kind, most likely," Schaeffer said. He looked over at Jacobson. "What do you think?"

"It's possible, but why a bag lady?"

"Totally anonymous," Schaeffer said, scratching his beard.

"Didn't Morley say there was a whole lot of hard stuff hitting the streets, from new sources? She could have been their runner. Remember those fifties we found in her shoe? Where would she get that kind of money?"

"Payoffs," Schaeffer offered. "For each job. Why not? It gives us an opening." He grabbed a cigarette from the pack on Jacobson's desk.

"You're ahead of me," Jacobson said, pulling the pack closer to himself.

"We'll put one of our own out on the street. See if they go for the bait. Chances are they'll stick to the same setup. It's a long shot but it can't hurt." He turned to Margaret. "Thanks a lot. That bit of information just might do it for us. 'Preciate it." She knew from the tone that this was his polite dismissal, but she didn't move. "Thank you," he repeated.

"What does it mean 'one of your own'?" she said, sitting back in her chair and crossing her legs. The two policemen looked at each other in silence. "An undercover policeman like Sergeant Schaeffer? Only dressed like a bag lady?" Margaret asked.

Schaeffer nodded. "Yeah, in case they need a new runner."

Margaret shook her head. "It won't work. Least not with a policewoman." She heard Schaeffer chuckle.

"Why not?"

"Because they're not old enough." She smiled up at him. "Sarah was over seventy."

"There are younger bag ladies."

"But if you use someone over seventy no one would ever suspect." She was surprised at herself. "And besides, it would help if you used someone who was a familiar figure in the neighborhood. May I?" She reached over for Jacobson's pack. "Know what I mean?"

He watched her slowly pull the cigarette out then light it.

Schaeffer sat back down. "What are you suggesting, that we use you?"

Margaret inhaled deeply. This is crazy, she thought. "Yes . . . wouldn't cost you anything and I'd be more believable than any policewoman. I've spent a lot of time on Broadway. I know the area. Besides," she grinned. "I know bag ladies. I'm around them every day. I know how they act, what they do."

Jacobson got up. "This is absurd."

"Wait a minute," Schaeffer said slowly. He looked at her more critically. "Maybe not. We use a lot of local informers. It's not that different. Only thing is"—he frowned—"what makes you so interested?"

She shrugged. "That's a good question. Guess I feel a little empty. I've spent too much time at the center handing out coffee. I think I could be doing more for them, for people like Sarah."

"Is that all?" Schaeffer watched her closely.

"And maybe a little bored too. Ever since Oscar died." She looked up at Jacobson. There was a silence. "My husband. When he died there was really nothing. You know how I spend my days when I'm not at the center?"

Jacobson shook his head.

"At my knitting group . . . in a kind of coma. Nothing ever changes. A lot of dull old women, dry, dusty, just like the old Victorian building we meet in. All they ever talk about is their grandchildren."

"You don't have any of your own?" Schaeffer asked.

Margaret looked at her hands. "No, Oscar and I couldn't . . ." She hesitated. Jacobson felt embarrassed. "So you see this would be kind of an adventure for me," she continued. "And I'd feel good about it, like I was being useful." She brightened when she looked up at Schaeffer. "It couldn't take too long. A few weeks maybe. I'd just tell everyone I was taking a trip, or something, get dressed up so they wouldn't recognize me on the street . . . like Rose."

"I don't know . . ." Schaeffer let a long ash fall to the floor. "It's more dangerous than knitting."

"Just to make contact and then tell you who they are?"

"Yes."

She shrugged it off. "You'll be around if I need you, right?"

Schaeffer glanced over at his partner. A smile was forming at the corners of his mouth. "What do you think?"

"Morley will never go for it. You know he hates getting civilians involved."

"Leave him to me. He's been on the carpet upstairs already because of all the coke that's floating in. He'll buy it. He'll buy anything that will get him off the hook. Only thing is, Mrs. Blinton, you got to look convincing or else they won't go for you."

"Call me Margaret. And don't worry," she said. "I think I've got just the right things."

"I'll have to clear it with the boss first," Schaeffer said. "I can't give you the go-ahead now. Where can I reach you?"

"Tomorrow afternoon at the center."

"And how soon after that could you start?"

"Right away, I suppose."

Schaeffer looked skeptically at the neat dress she was wearing. "We'll get in touch with you. Meanwhile, think it over. I'm not sure you know what you might be getting yourself into, and who knows, when you leave here you might want to change your mind."

"Oh, no," Margaret said, getting up to leave. "I'm quite sure it will be all right. I've been around for a while, you know, and I think you might just find me useful." She paused at the door to wave good-bye. "Until tomorrow," she called as she walked down the hall, leaving Jacobson and Schaeffer stunned and silent.

Lieutenant Sam Morley was seated behind a desk crammed full with papers. On the wall were pictures of him in earlier days, various poses with other uniformed men, and also a *Daily News* clipping of him holding a young, dazed-looking child in his arms. He had been heavier then, more muscular, but the face was the same, the square chin still as prominent, though the hair had grayed.

Schaeffer slouched down in the chair across from him. "You know I'm right, Sam," he said. "Why fight it?"

Morley pointed a finger at him. "Because I'm running this investigation, not you. Just because you come up with some crazy dame that wants a few kicks doesn't mean I gotta go for it."

"She's not crazy."

"She's old enough to be my mother. That's crazy!" He raised his voice. "You're putting her on the street like a sitting duck. You know what it's like out there. Besides, she doesn't know a goddamn thing about undercover work."

"She doesn't need to know much. Come on, boss. All she's gotta do is make contact. What's that? Playing dumb for a coupla days. They might not even get to her."

"I still don't like it. She could blow the whole operation."

"You got something better? Robbins is on your tail night and day with this cocaine thing. What else you got cooking? All the regular informers are out in left field on this one."

"Yeah, yeah." Morley leaned back.

Schaeffer lit a cigarette. "No one's approached me yet. We gotta use her. She seems like a natural. But," Schaeffer sighed, "it's your neck not mine."

"Yeah, well if we use her and she blows it, it's yours, understand. Your idea, your responsibility."

Schaeffer sat up and smiled.

Morley was silent for a minute.

"What's her name?"

"Margaret Binton."

"She ready to go?"

Schaeffer nodded.

Morley stood up. "I don't like it one goddamn bit though."

"You will." Schaeffer grinned. "You'll see."


Margaret could hardly conceal her excitement when she was called to the phone the next afternoon.

"Good news," Schaeffer began. "You're on."

"Really? You mean right away?"

"Yes, right away."

She chuckled. "I'll have to tell them here."

"All right, see you later. Just start out as soon as you're ready. I'll find you."

She put the phone down slowly and then went to find the director. She explained that her nephew, who lived out of town, was very ill and that she would have to go take care of him. Margaret thought it a feeble excuse as she left the office, but the director had seemed to take it as truth. Margaret walked home at a brisk pace, excited at the prospect of an interesting afternoon.

After a quick tea and sandwich Margaret opened her closet and poked between the hangers. She reminisced about the days when as a child she had rummaged through her mother's trunks, dressing up and parading through the neighborhood for all to see. But now, she shouldn't change too drastically. Not at first. If her friends spotted her, they might begin to wonder.

She fished out her oldest pair of shoes. The heels were worn down, the leather horribly scuffed and in need of polish. The tips turned up to the ceiling. "As long as they're comfortable," she sighed, wiggling her toes. She would have to do a lot of walking. An old green dress hung at the back, forgotten for years. It needed its hem re-stitched. Perfect. She grabbed the arms and stretched them out at her sides. It seemed small, but she struggled into it and, after opening a few more boxes and dodging some dim shapes that fell off the shelf, found a faded red sweater. It brought back memories of Oscar. It had been his favorite. She brought it over to the window but couldn't find any holes in it and debated whether or not to cut into the elbow. She couldn't bring herself to do it and decided instead on two sweaters, the outer one buttoned askew. Her old yellow cardigan would be just right. "The layered, lumpy look," she said, clowning in front of the full-length mirror. She bent over slowly and pulled out two socks, one white and one gray, then yanked them on and rolled down the tops. They would do, she decided, as her eyes traveled the length of her reflection, taking in her new image. She was almost satisfied, but something was out of place. She didn't quite look the part and it would be enough to make her fail. She just didn't look like Rose or Sarah. "Now what . . ." She studied herself closer in the mirror. "Ah, yes, hair."

Margaret had always pinned her hair up neatly in a bun, a habit of twenty years. She slowly pulled a few strands out of place but they looked too deliberate, contrived. She took out the long hat pin and let her gray hair fall down her back but it was still wrong, and it felt uncomfortable. She quickly pinned her hair back up and covered her head with a loose scarf, letting the edge come just above her eyes. She tightened the knot, walked to her cleaning closet, pulled out four paper shopping bags, and then puffed them out as she stood by the window. All ready, she thought, looking down into the street. For the first time she felt nervous. She hadn't even stopped to think what poking into garbage cans would be like, not to mention making contact with a bunch of murderers. She took a deep breath, crossed her tiny apartment, and headed out for the first time as a bag lady.

Schaeffer leaned against the rough limestone of the stoop and lifted his head in a slow arc. The act was studied. He'd learned it on his own, off duty, watching drunks and trying it out on street corners around the city. He glanced at the roof, his eyes half closed, then slowly lowered his head and continued watching the front door. She'd be coming out soon.

He shifted position from one foot to the other, searched his pockets for his old toothpick and stuck it in his mouth.

He straightened slightly as the door opened across the street. An old woman emerged from Margaret's building and walked toward Riverside Drive. Too thin to be Margaret, Schaeffer thought, slumping back into place.

The door opened again. Schaeffer smiled. She'd done pretty well. Even the walk. He watched carefully. He picked up the slightest nod of recognition from her, but gave none in return and waited until she reached the end of the block before stepping out after her.

# Two

MARGARET FELT EXPOSED, BUT SHE
knew that combing the side streets would be a waste of
time. If she wanted to be approached, she would have to
stay on Broadway.

At first, she could barely control her nerves. She would
approach a garbage can and glance around to see if anyone
recognized her. She would stick her hand into the bin,
quickly rummage around, and walk away, her empty bags
fluttering in the wind. Each time she felt like a shoplifter,
sneaking away with feelings of guilt and triumph, but her
bags remained empty, except for a newspaper or two.

By five o'clock she was exhausted. Her feet throbbed
and her eyes were sore from scrutinizing every passer-by.
She had walked from Eighty-first Street to Ninety-second,
and back down to Eighty-fifth. She sat down on a traffic
island bench and closed her eyes. Her head was swirling
with visions of orange peels, greasy Big Mac containers,
and mounds of crumpled paper.

"How's it going, Margaret?"

She jumped to the edge of the bench, panicked that the
murderers had found her already.

"Oh, it's you."

Sergeant Schaeffer sat at the other end, his body
slouched, his eyes focussed straight ahead. His clothes and

beard looked even more disheveled than they had yesterday morning.

"How am I doing?" she mumbled.

"Well, you look great. I'd give you an Academy Award for best costume design." His voice trailed off and he began to cough.

The light changed and pedestrians swarmed across the island. When traffic began again three people were left waiting to cross. One of them looked over at Margaret and Schaeffer and shook her head, pulling her handbag closer to her side, anxious for the light to change.

"See, I told you," Schaeffer said softly, once the pedestrians had gone. "We're the real thing."

"Hope it doesn't change me," Margaret sighed. "I'll begin to expect handouts."

"Nothing wrong with that," he said lightheartedly. "Listen, I got one complaint."

She looked over at him. "Yes? About me?"

"Uh huh. You've got to be a little less wary of those cans." He waited, "I mean, it looks to me like you were afraid of setting off a bomb or something. You're too delicate."

"It's awkward. They smell."

"I know, but if you want to be convincing you've got to really dig down deep."

"But what if a friend comes by?"

"You can't worry about it. Just shove your hand down."

"Here, let me show you." He led Margaret across the street to a can and then thrust his arm to the bottom. He looked up at Margaret. "They don't want someone who's only going to sift through the top."

She watched, fidgeting, her fists tight around the handles of her bags.

"See," Schaeffer said, pulling out a plastic spoon. "Pretend this is sterling silver."

"That's pretty hard." Margaret laughed.

"So, okay, not a silver spoon." Schaeffer reached into the can and pulled out a piece of paper. "How about a ticket to Miami Beach? Anything . . ." Schaeffer said, rubbing his hands on his pants legs. "Anything that will make you want to go through the whole can. Why don't you try it now?"

"Now?"

"Yeah, why not? Go on." Schaeffer could sense she was hesitating. "Listen," he said. "I put twenty dollars in one of the four cans on this block. I want to see you find it."

"What is this, a game?" Margaret asked.

"Okay," he said. "Think of it that way."

Schaeffer crossed the street and casually leaned against a lamppost, watching her out of the corner of his eye.

Margaret found a can farther down the block and began fumbling with the papers. She got down as far as she could reach, and when she hadn't found anything, stood up and cleaned off her arms with a scrap of paper. She glanced over at Schaeffer, a sour scowl on her face. She waited for some people to pass and then walked over to another full can. A mop handle protruded from the top and she lifted it out and looked it over, remembering she had wanted to buy a new one. She leaned her prize against the container and, at the thought of having just saved three dollars, started digging deeper.

Something wet brushed against her hand and she jerked up her arm. It was only an apple core, but the sensation had frightened her. She'd seen rats dart into cans before, and she shuddered at the thought of touching one. She took a deep breath and prepared for a new attack. Her eye spotted something green, and, thrilled at the prospect, she carefully slid her hand past the apple core, finally pinching a piece of paper between two fingers. It felt like a new bill. She inched her fingers farther down.

"Hey. Hullo, Margaret."

"It was a woman's voice. Margaret froze.

"What ya doin'?"

Margaret looked up into Rose's face and tried to crumple the bill into her palm as quickly as she could.

"Oh, Rose, you frightened me," Margaret said as she stood up. "Isn't it funny. I just dropped a letter in here by mistake. So awful, from an old friend who moved away."

She cleared her throat. "I realized too late that it had a new return address on it."

"Here, lemme," Rose offered. "You don't wanna dirty your pretty sweaters."

"No, that's all right," Margaret said. She was relieved that Rose hadn't noticed the change in her appearance. "She'll probably get in touch with me again."

"Sure?"

"Yeah." Margaret hesitated. "Well Rose. How are things at the center?"

"Same." Rose eyed the mop handle Margaret had leaned against the can. She went over to inspect it and then stuck it into one of her bags.

"Well, I've got to go now," Margaret said, somewhat miffed. "I guess I'll see you soon." She looked over her shoulder but Schaeffer had gone.

Rose nodded and started to sift through the can, stopping long enough to wave good-bye as Margaret started across the street.

For the next week Margaret walked the Upper West Side streets in search of imaginary prizes. She was enjoying herself and she attacked every can she approached with enough aggression to make her first day's efforts look . . . amateurish. Her sweater had even developed several small rips. She was getting used to the strain and stayed out longer; her bags filled up and nearly overflowed. Each night she carefully unloaded her booty onto her kitchen table. One prize was a book of *New York Times* crossword puzzles. Its owner had apparently attempted two or three and had given up in disgust. Amateur, she had thought, in above his head. She had also found an Agatha Christie paperback, a new one which she hadn't yet read, and a small picture frame. The glass was broken but could easily be replaced.

A second inadvertent meeting with Rose produced some useful information. Rose told her that a man had approached her that morning. He'd asked if she wanted a job. "Well," she had reported, "I was wonderin', you know, I mean what kinda work's he thinkin' I could do. So's I asked him straight out what sorta work an' he says somethin' 'bout deliverin' things. Told him right there I'm gonna be no glorified messenger boy. Besides," she added with a wink, "don't need much more money now. So's I gives him a look he won't soon forget."

"That's one relief," Schaeffer said after hearing the story. "Morley and I were worried that they might approach someone else before they get to you. At least we know they haven't found anyone yet. Hang on for a little longer. I'm sure they'll contact you. Just keep it up. You're a star degenerate."

Margaret had come to rely on Schaeffer. At first she thought he would only offer an occasional checkpoint but after the first day she realized he could help much more. She felt reassured that he was devoting the whole day to the case and she often noticed him a block away, casually watching her. Sometimes he even walked on the same block, keeping well behind.

Margaret became more edgy as the second week began. She was also more observant of passers-by, hoping to recognize a recurrent face, but no one paid her any special attention. It was disheartening.

Schaeffer tried to encourage her when he saw her losing interest. He figured on another two days before she'd turn in her bags, but Margaret gathered her energy and assured Schaeffer she would work until the end of the week.

Friday morning was cold and rainy and only a few people were on the streets, all hurrying from one place to another. Margaret would normally have stayed home, watching TV and drinking tea, and by 11:30 she was chilled and fed up. She hadn't even found anything worth taking home. She walked into Squire's and collapsed into a booth, scattering the half-filled bags at her feet. She watched the rain come, harder every minute, bouncing off the pavement, scissoring the air. I should quit now, she thought, imagining herself, the soaking wet bag lady, struggling with her cache into a taxi and being chauffeured the eight blocks home.

"Lousy day out, ain't it?"

Margaret looked up as a man slid into her booth and sat across from her. "Don't mind, do you? The other booths were full."

"No," Margaret replied. "I'll be leaving soon anyway."

"Why don't you wait till it stops?"

Margaret stiffened. "It'll be a while—besides, they need the booth and I don't have enough money to keep ordering muffins all day." She wasn't sure about him. He could be just a friendly guy anxious for lunch, but if this was the contact, she had given him an opening.

He motioned for the waitress and ordered a coffee and two muffins. "On me," he said. "You look like you could use another."

They sat in silence for a few minutes until his coffee came. Margaret glanced out the window and caught the man's reflection. His height was above average although it was hard to tell with him sitting down. About forty, maybe forty-five, she thought, dark hair and darkish complexion. She could hear herself reeling the description off to Schaeffer. Expensive coat, shirt open about six or seven inches. She thought of the rain dripping down his hairy chest. A gold chain hung around his neck, a shark's tooth dangling at the end. She pictured him driving a white Cadillac convertible with the top down, elbow hanging out the window. He could have only one reason to be in this coffee shop eating English muffins with her.

"Been outdoors today?" he asked, looking at her wet raincoat.

"Sure." She'd been trying to change her way of talking, picking up from Schaeffer and keeping her conversations with Rose in mind. "Shoulda stayed home—arthritis acts up in this weather."

"Whadda you go out for then? Work or pleasure?"

"Nah, too old to work. Couldn't do nothin'." She ripped off a bite of the muffin and kept talking with her mouth full, chewing between words, sipping tea now and then to keep the bread from getting stuck. "I just go out and snoop about. See what's around. Keeps my busy."

"Must be nice to not worry about money." He sat back and grinned. More like a leer, she thought.

"You kiddin'? Whadda ya think—I own a bank or somethin'? That's a laugh, mister. If I had money, you think I'd be here? You're baloney. I'd be down in Miami." She stopped to swallow some tea.

"You could be." He leaned forward.

"Hey?" She squinted at him, moving her tongue around her gums to free a lump of bread.

"I said you could be. You could make a little extra if you wanted to." He scanned the neighboring booths. "Go anywhere you like."

"Yeah. How? Walkin' dogs?" She leaned down under the table to scratch her leg.

"I'm sure we could arrange for a little work if you were interested." He looked around the cafeteria and then back at her. "Nothing too risky," he said softly, staring closely at her, sizing her up.

Margaret shifted a little in her chair. "I don't know, mister. Sounds a little funny. Know what I mean?" She took another bite and chewed for a minute, training her eyes on the table.

He smiled and leaned closer, folding his hands in front of him before he looked up at her. "We need someone to deliver things around the area."

"What kinda things?" Margaret was almost shouting, studying him all the while, trying to remember his face.

He put a finger to his lips to quiet her down.

"Just paychecks."

She waited a few moments. "Nah. At my age I can't go chasing around like that.

"No, no. No chasing around. A couple trips a week, that's all."

"Yeah?" She gave him a hard look.

"Fifty dollars a shot."

She whistled. "That's not a little money, mister."

"One, maybe two times a week. In no time you could take a vacation in Miami."

"I'll say." She took another sip of her tea. "You sure this is kosher?" she said squinting.

"Nothing to worry about—guaranteed safe." He hunched up his shoulders, pulling the lapels closer to his neck. He could sense she was wavering.

A full minute passed before Margaret spoke again. "So, what's the deal?" she said softly, moving her face close to his across the table.

"You gotta phone?"

"Nah, you kiddin'? I can barely pay my rent."

He reached into his pocket and handed her a fifty-dollar bill. "Call up the phone company and get them to install one in your place. This'll cover it."

"How will you get my number? You don't even know my name."

He smiled at her. "Mrs. Binton, you're not dealing with a bunch of amateurs."

"Oh," she said. "What happens then?"

"Then you wait. We'll call you. Just make sure you're home at ten in the morning."

"What morning?"

"Every morning until you hear from us. That fifty also buys some of your time."

"And that's it?"

"That's all for now. Uh, of course, this is a private matter. You know, just between you and me. I wouldn't go mentioning it to any of your friends if I were you."

"Don't worry. I need the money."

"Another thing. Don't write anything down. Just keep the information in your head." He pulled out a five-dollar bill and laid it on the table. "I think we're gonna get along just fine. Have some more muffins if you want—stay all afternoon." He winked at her, slid out of the booth, and left.

Margaret looked down at the money next to her empty plate. It was all over. She couldn't wait to tell Schaeffer. She looked out the window and wondered if she should keep the rendezvous. She would probably look very suspicious sitting in the rain and decided she would skip it. He'd get in touch with her somehow. She felt elated. It had worked. Enough of this old-lady food, she sighed, calling the waitress over and ordering their largest hamburger. "Don't forget the onions," she called and sat back to watch the rain.

Schaeffer didn't think Margaret would be out in the rain but he kept his eyes open, just in case, stopping in doorway after doorway to dry off a bit. Then he spotted her through the window of Squire's Coffee Shop. She was eating alone, and he pressed his nose to the glass and grinned. When she finally glanced up at him he knew something had happened. She looked both upset and excited at the same time.

He moved away quickly, trying to think of a discreet way of contacting her. After a few minutes he walked into the coffee shop and ordered coffee while he scribbled "New Yorker Theater/balcony" on a napkin. It was only two blocks away.

Margaret had seen Schaeffer come in, but she waited patiently while he finished his coffee. After a short time he got up and tossed the crumpled napkin onto her table as he walked out.

Schaeffer found an empty row of seats to the rear of the balcony and chose a spot near the wall. Bad choice, he thought after settling down to watch the screen. *Suspicion*, an old Hitchcock. Schaeffer had eaten, slept, and drunk Hitchcock for two years in college.

Margaret arrived a few minutes later while Cary Grant was arguing with Joan Fontaine. There were subtle undertones of menace in his language, unspoken threats. Margaret leaned closer and whispered, "Watch the glass."

"Oh, you know?"

She nodded. "I love Hitchcock. I think I've seen them all. You know about the lightbulb?"

"Yeah. In the glass of milk. Makes it look more fatal." He smiled at her. "Want to watch or talk?"

She glanced quickly at the screen. "This can't wait."

Margaret told Schaeffer about her meeting.

"You still want to go through with it?" he asked after she had finished.

"Sure. What else do I have to do except serve coffee at the center and go to my knitting group. Anyway, I had fun today and I think *I* could pull it off. I was a little nervous but he didn't suspect." Margaret smiled. "When I'm into the scheme a bit I'll be a natural. Don't worry."

Schaeffer had become very fond of Margaret in the past two weeks and was apprehensive about the man she had described to him. His type would try anything.

"Just do what they say. We'll have full surveillance on you so you shouldn't get into too much trouble. When they call with the drop-off points, leave a message. Tell us the location. We should know by following you, but we can't risk too close a tail."

"Where should I leave it?"

"I checked out your building last week. Where the garbage is kept in the back there's a small U-shaped air vent —near a drain. You can't miss it. Just tape a note inside the vent with the address. It's safe. No one will see it there but be sure you're alone when you do it."

She nodded.

"We'll follow up. Most likely the money is going to one person. When we build up enough of a case, we'll bust them. Then you can go back to your pigeons."

"I had a better offer a half hour ago."

He smiled. "Oh, yes, I think we should meet only once in a while. I'll find you. Now that they've contacted you, they may be keeping a close watch on." He touched her arm and squeezed it gently, wondering if he should really get her involved with that man.

Margaret looked over at him and smiled. "Let's hope it works," she whispered, patting his knee. "Then we can come back here for more Hitchcock."

He thought for a moment. "We have to get you down to the precinct to look over the mug books, but you just can't walk in off the street. It's too risky. We'll think of something. Tomorrow around eleven A.M., while he's still fresh in your mind." He got up to go. "Good luck. Don't forget to call the phone company."

"I won't," she whispered. "Soon as I see the end of the movie."

# Three

MAX DAKER LEANED BACK IN HIS SWIVEL chair and put his feet on the desk. Cotlin stood in front of him, surveying the Gucci shoes, the miles of mahogany, the tightly creased gabardine trousers. Sunlight streamed in through the wall of windows, backlighting Daker's tinted gray hair and throwing harsh shadows onto his face. Cotlin squinted a bit to bring his boss's face into focus.

"I understand you got another person for the drops," Daker said.

"Yeah," Cotlin nodded. "I approached two or three and got lucky on the third."

"No nonsense this time. We can't afford another screw-up like the last one." Daker reached for his gold pen and twirled it in his fingers. "We've got a goddamn good thing going here and I don't want to blow it on account of some old bitch gets nervous or greedy." He pointed the pen toward Cotlin. "You run a check on her?"

Cotlin shifted position. "Sure. Name is Margaret Binton, lives at Eighty-first and Broadway, a side building. She's a widow." He pulled a piece of paper from his jacket pocket, stopping to adjust the gold chain around his neck before he opened the envelope. "She's lived in the same apartment for over fifteen years. People know her. She lives off Social Security and has been hitting the streets regularly since I spotted her."

"How long?" Daker lifted one shoe into the air to admire the shine.

"What?" Cotlin hated Daker's question routine. He was tired of standing.

"How long before that had she been on the streets?"

"Long time, I guess," Cotlin said, letting out his breath. Goddamn Daker, he thought. Should trust me by now, the son-of-a-bitch. Cotlin stuffed the envelope into his pocket. "I found some old guy that claims he's seen her hanging around Broadway for years."

"What else?" Daker's voice was cold and mechanical.

"What else?" he repeated, staring Cotlin full in the face.

"I slipped into her apartment on Wednesday. One room. You should have seen all the crap lying around."

"Think she could be a plant?"

"Nah. You shoulda seen her eyes light up when I flashed that fifty. Anyway, there's no reason for the cops to be suspicious. That Feiner woman, you know, Mund made it look like a robbery. Old lady's found murdered in some goddamn tenement, what else could it be . . . a jealous lover?" He laughed but stopped abruptly when he noticed that Daker hadn't joined him. He was sure Margaret Binton was nothing like Sarah Feiner. Somehow she had struck him as the perfect find, a natural.

"Sounds okay." Daker stood up and turned to the windows. "Just the same," he said, "for the first week or two I want her watched. She says hello to a cop on the sidewalk and that's it. She starts acting suspicious in any way and we drop her. You got it? I'm taking no chances. I got to where I am because I'm careful." He paused. "In fact, I want you to do a week of dummy drops and watch the decoy. Pick someone in the Seventies. After a few drops we'll know. Till then, pretend she's hot. And put Mund on it right away. If you talk to her, I want you off the phone in thirty seconds. Call from a pay phone."

Daker started to sift through some papers on his desk, the signal for Cotlin to leave.

# Four

MARGARET SAT DOWN WITH HER *NEW York Times* crossword book after she came home from the movies. She had finished only the first six but turned to the middle of the book to find a more difficult puzzle.

She quickly fillled in one across, "bargello pattern." The rest of the puzzle was slow going, and after an hour she had completed only half of it and her eyes were sore. A little rusty, she thought, yawning as she closed the book. She had never left a puzzle unfinished and promised herself that she would complete it the next day.

Margaret woke early and lingered over a cup of black coffee. She always took it with milk, but she had run out and wondered whether or not she could risk going to the store. Schaeffer would be coming for her at 11:00. He hadn't told her how long it would take to look at the mug books, she should also set aside some time to poke around in the cans, for appearance's sake. She didn't know how she could find time for everything, but another sip of the bitter coffee convinced her to go out for the milk. She would worry about scavenging later.

The Grand Union was always crowded on Saturday mornings. Margaret dressed in the same costume she had worn since she had started her undercover work. She had gotten used to it, but she felt the stares of the weekend shoppers. If they only knew, she thought as she pushed her wire cart down the cluttered aisles.

She was careful to choose only a few simple, inexpensive items, aware that to splurge would arouse suspicion if she was under surveillance. Old-lady food again, she thought disgustedly.

Margaret lost her footing when someone bumped her from behind.

"You should watch where you're going," she snapped.

"Excuse me," said the man. "I was looking for the soups." He examined her carefully, establishing her features in his mind. From the looks of her, she wouldn't be hard to deal with if she turned out to be another of Cotlin's filching recruits, Mund thought, watching as Margaret hurried down the aisle. I wouldn't have picked her though, he thought as he followed her out of the store. When she turned into her building, he waited across the street to see what she would do.

When Margaret arrived home at 10:30, she surveyed her little hoard and shrugged her shoulders. None of it looked very appetizing. She put her groceries away and sat down to wait for Schaeffer.

By 11:15 no one had come. She tried to finish her puzzle but put it down after five minutes. She was nervous and her mind kept trying to focus on the man with the shark's-tooth necklace. She was afraid she might have forgotten his face.

The street noises drifted up to her and made her feel even more anxious. If he didn't come soon she wouldn't have time to go out on the streets.

A siren wailed off in the distance. Another mugging, she thought. The cops have their hands full with this neighborhood. As she watched out her window, the sirens got louder, piercing through the other noise from the street. She peered over the window sill and saw the ambulance turn down her street.

A heart attack, she mused. They shouldn't let old people live in walk-ups. It ought to be in the lease. The siren stopped but the lights continued to flash until the vehicle stopped in front of her building. After a minute she heard a knock on her door.

Well, what a surprise, she laughed. I think I'm about to become very ill.

The prospect of a ride through the city in an ambulance was exciting. The attendant wrapped gauze bandages around her head and after ten minutes it began to itch. She was strapped to a stretcher and a heavy blanket was pulled up to her chin. She sensed the gawking spectators when she was rushed out of the building, but fortunately the attendants did a good job of keeping them back. She heard one of them yell, "Come on, don't crowd, he's in shock. Give him room." She smiled behind her bandages.

When the ambulance arrived at a nearby hospital, she was transferred into the emergency area and was wheeled into a side room. Someone undid the straps and started to unwind the bandages. The room was quiet except for a few hospital sounds that filtered in from the wards down the hall. Margaret savored the cool air that promised to soothe her face. She could feel it coming through the last layers of gauze and wanted to put her hands to her head and rip them off herself, but Schaeffer beat her to it. Margaret rubbed her forehead and cheeks and Schaeffer grinned at her from the end of the stretcher as he pulled off the shirt of his hospital uniform.

"Remarkable recovery. Sorry we had to truss you up like this, but we wanted to be extra careful. Oh, we also left a man in your apartment. He'll just turn on the TV and walk around a lot. Soon's you get back he'll leave through the service entrance."

"Do you think anybody was watching?"

"Probably," Schaeffer said. "But since they don't really suspect you, they're not going to go out on a limb and get too close. We gave a story to the super in case someone was watching the building and wanted to find out who was sick."

They walked out of the side entrance, stepped into an unmarked car, and drove into the precinct garage.

Sergeant Schaeffer took Margaret to Morley's office and they led her to the room with the mug books.

"Take your time," Morley said. "If you see anybody that even resembles your man, pull him out. Remember, once he could have had a mustache or a different hair style." He walked to the door. "I'll be in my office if you need me. Schaeffer, stay with Margaret and help her with the books, and both of you see me before you leave."

Margaret opened the first book and began to scrutinize each face. There were four books on the table and she paled at the thought of having to look through them all. At first she concentrated on details. The closeness of the eyes, the shape of the nose. It was slow going, and as she proceeded her criteria changed. She took one look at the face and if it did anything to her she looked more closely. Otherwise she passed on to the next page. Schaeffer went out once in a while to get tea and doughnuts and put each book away after she had finished with it. After four hours, she sat back and rubbed her eyes.

"Is that it?" she asked.

"Every single one." Schaeffer looked down at the four faces she had picked out. "Do you have any special feelings about any of them?"

"Not really. I don't think he's in there, but they look like him . . . maybe."

"Well, there's always a chance. Hold on a minute while I run these through." He made a quick phone call and then got up to go.

"I never realized how many criminals there were in New York," she said. "Some of them look so nice. You'd never suspect."

"Amazing, huh?"

Schaeffer helped her up and the two of them walked down to Morley's office.

"Find anything?" Morley asked as they entered.

"Four possibles. Ricciardi is checking on them now. I told him to phone me here." He looked over at Margaret.

"She's a real plugger. I've seen people give up after two books."

Morley smiled. Too soon for applause, he thought. The phone rang and he picked it up and scribbled some notes on a pad. When he had hung up he ripped off the sheet and leaned back in his chair.

"Willy Moscovy's up at Greenhaven. Been there three years on a fraud conviction. Charlie Evans is in Attica. You remember, he was one of the guys you boys got on the Simmons case." Schaeffer nodded.

"Bruno Locatelli is out, but he's all wrong. The guy is a two-bit robber. Break and entry. It's out of his depth." He looked over at Margaret. "Did your man have a noticeable accent?"

"No." She hesitated. "Well, maybe from the Bronx." She looked at Schaeffer. "You know, like William Bendix in *Lifeboat*." Schaeffer chuckled.

"So then Locatelli's out for sure. That leaves us with Chuck Marlen. Convicted in sixty-eight for pushing dope, served four years on a four-to-eight and was paroled for good behavior. His latest parole report had him moving to Texas." He looked at Schaeffer. "He's a maybe." Morley dialed a number and asked for a check on Texas. "What do you think, Margaret?"

"Who can tell from those mug shots?" She shrugged her shoulders. "They'd make Omar Sharif look like Mickey Rooney. It could be him, but then again I didn't react strongly to any of them, you know...down here." She patted her stomach. "I have a feeling if it was him I'd know it."

Morley reached into his coat pocket and pulled out a pack of cigarettes. He took one out and lit it. "There's one more thing. Now that you've made contact, it's going to get rough." He rose and stood next to Margaret's chair. "I want you to be extra careful and do everything they tell you to. The deeper you fall in with them, the more dangerous it is for you. If you feel they are onto you, let us know. We'll get you out." He smiled at her. "Sergeant Schaeffer here has taken a shine to you. So be careful."

"I'll try." All this talk made her nervous. She reached for one of Morley's cigarettes.

The lieutenant walked back to his chair.

"You know about the air vent. If you've left us a message, carry your Bowery bag, the one with Joe DiMaggio on it. If not, leave it home. Also, contact Schaeffer only if you have to, and if we have to get in touch with you, we'll write a note in a copy of *Psychology Today* and leave it in the can at Eighty-seventh and West End, northeast corner."

"Yes, Officer."

"Check it every day. If you see that magazine, check page twelve. If it's from us, there will be a note there. After you've read the note, throw the magazine back." He took a drag on his cigarette. "This is probably the last time I'll see you until we make an arrest. The ambulance routine is out. In fact, any routine would be suspicious." He held out his hand. "Schaeffer will take you back. The master of disguise has a new costume for you to wear in case their tail hasn't tired of waiting." He squeezed her hand. "Good luck."

Margaret laughed. "That's all I hear around here."

# Five

ON SUNDAY, MARGARET WENT TO THE
alley behind her building to familiarize herself with the air
vent. It was well hidden and fairly inaccessible from the
street. She continued with her rounds that afternoon and on
Tuesday morning a man came to install a phone in her
apartment.

The first call came on Thursday. It sounded like the man
she'd met at Squire's. She'd heard traffic in the back-
ground, and he spoke slowly to make sure she understood.
"Mrs. Binton, listen carefully. There's some blue socks in
the garbage can at Eighty-eighth and Amsterdam, north-
west corner. There's an envelope and a fifty inside one of
them. The fifty's for you. The envelope goes to Mr. S.
Rudley at 155 West Seventh-fifth Street. Drop it in his
mailbox. Got it?"

"Funny place to pick up money."

"Why do you think we got you?"

She was about to say something when the phone went
dead. "His manners have deteriorated," she said aloud. She
scribbled the name and address on a piece of paper and five
minutes later she had stuck it to the inside of the air vent
and was on her way to Eighty-eighth Street. She made sure
Joe DiMaggio's face was visible on her Bowery bag.

Cotlin started following Margaret as soon as she left her

building. He was driving with one eye on the rearview mirror in case a police car started down the block.

Schaeffer was staked out in a room across the street from Margaret's. He had rented the place the same afternoon they had met at the movie. It had an excellent view of Margaret's building and the entire street. Since Margaret had gotten her phone, he had gone through about two hundred hands of solitaire but had won only two. Depressing odds, he thought as he watched Margaret's building. He'd have to find something else to do.

He was almost relieved when he saw Margaret leave her building with the Bowery bag. He waited two or three minutes to make sure no one was following her and called Morley on his radio to tell him that they had had a contact.

It didn't take Margaret long to find the socks. They were under a newspaper about a third of the way down, new, like Rose's shirt. Rose's money had been loose, but this was in a plain sealed envelope. She found a crumpled $50 in the toe, stuffed it into one of her bags, and slipped the envelope under her sweater sleeve, as she did with her handkerchiefs. This is a cinch, she thought as she started toward the drop-off point.

Beautiful pickup, Cotlin grinned as he started his car again to follow Margaret down the street. Even better than Sarah Feiner. Natural, he smiled to himself. A real winner this time.

Schaeffer checked the police special strapped to his calf before leaving his apartment. He then went across the street and snuck into Margaret's alley with the key he'd made for the gate. The note tore a bit when he pulled it from the vent, but he pieced it together, and after memorizing the information, took out a match and burned it. He'd catch up with her between the pick-up and drop-off. He didn't expect anything to happen, but he wanted to keep an eye on her just the same. At the first phone booth he saw, he called the details in to Morley and then stationed himself in the corner Laundromat at Seventy-eighth and Amsterdam. He didn't have to wait more than four minutes before Margaret passed by.

She turned east on Seventy-fifth Street until she came to 155, a renovated five-story walk-up. The front door opened onto a tiny vestibule lined with intercom buzzers and mailboxes. She stuffed the envelope into S. Rudley's slot and left.

So, that was it. Her first drop. She could see why Sarah had been willing to continue with the scheme. Easy. In less than half an hour she had made $50. Too bad it's illegal, she thought.

By the time Schaeffer arrived at Seventy-fifth, Margaret was already leaving 155. She was walking toward him and they passed each other without giving any sign of recognition, but when he turned around to check on Margaret, she was nowhere in sight.

Cotlin had planned to stick to her until she got home. For the first few times anyway. Mund had been switched to watching Rudley's place. That will be boring. Cotlin laughed. A whole week waiting for cops that ain't never coming. He stopped for a red light at Seventy-eighth Street. Wish I could be there when this guy Rudley opens his mail, he chuckled. A blank envelope with eight blank pieces of paper. Drive the son-of-a-bitch crazy.

Schaeffer finally saw Margaret a block ahead of him. She was still walking quickly and he tried to keep pace with her. Broadway was bumper to bumper and every now and then he lost sight of her when the traffic blocked the intersection. Schaeffer stopped following her at Eighty-first Street when he saw her turn into her block, and he headed right for the precinct. The name Rudley meant something to him, but he had no idea what.

Cotlin caught up with Margaret as she was entering her building. He waited another few minutes before driving back to the office to tell Daker. Christ, he thought, that guy wouldn't trust his own mother.

Morley was busy reading the report on Marlen when Schaeffer walked in.

"Marlen hasn't left Texas for six months. Works in a diner five days a week in Austin. Employer says he's a steady worker. The Austin P.D. says he stays close to home. As far as I'm concerned that's it. He could be pulling something down there, but I don't think he's our man."

"I didn't think it would be that easy," Schaeffer said, scratching his beard. "Must be a new operation. They wouldn't use a mug with a record for their contact man."

Morley nodded and leaned back. "Where's Margaret?"

"Back home."

"Everything go okay?"

"Yeah, no problem." He paused. "Did you check on Rudley?"

"The only thing I can tell so far is he doesn't have a record. You want to wait?"

"No." Schaeffer got up. "I'm going to grab a bite. See you later."

He turned and closed the door softly behind him. All the way to the diner, he tried to remember where he had heard the name "Rudley" before. During lunch he tried making connections and cross references. Relatives' friends, characters in stories he had read, old girlfriend's father, TV characters. It went on and on.

At one o'clock he was back in Morley's office looking over the report on Rudley. It was dull reading.

"Crazy, huh?" Schaeffer asked.

"Not at all," Morley said. "It's beautiful. They get some completely innocent guy with no record, cut him in for a little money, and use him as a collection point. It's really a double drop. It's smart. Adds another link between the operation and us. If they feel we're on to the garbage pickups, they just remove Mr. Rudley and they're in the clear."

"What if their second drop wasn't so innocent and took a quick trip to Mexico with all that lovely cash?" Schaeffer asked, lighting one of Morley's cigarettes.

"First of all, he'd probably wind up on the floor in some Mexican bathroom. Secondly, they would probably make it worth his while." Morley slapped the report down on his desk.

"Christ, this guy Rudley is a civil engineer," Schaeffer protested. "They make good money."

Morley took the cigarette from Schaeffer. "No matter. I want him tailed. Loosely, but I want a list of everyone he sees. We can't move on him too soon or we'll wind up with nothing. Let's wait and see what happens."

"How long?"

"A week. Let's give him a week to make contact. We can't wait longer than that." Morley took another puff and crushed the cigarette out. "You stay with Mom. I'll put someone else on Rudley."

Schaeffer knew everything was moving too fast. It was just too easy.

# Six

MARGARET MADE FOUR MORE DROPS
during the week. They were all picked up in the same general area and were all delivered to S. Rudley. Schaeffer
followed. He was still unable to place the name Rudley,
but it bothered him, and he thought about it every waking
moment.

Cotlin followed also, but he gave up after two days. He
was convinced she was clean. Mund stayed at his post,
waiting for a bust on Rudley. He felt that there was something wrong about Margaret, but he still didn't have a clue.

Morley had three plainclothesmen covering Rudley. He
rotated the assignments every day to ensure against boredom. Jacobson was with the frankfurter wagon on the
corner. When he took a break, Benson watched from a TV
repair van parked about forty yards down the block. At
night they used an unmarked panel truck. When Rudley
left, Staunton followed.

Rudley never changed his schedule. Out by eight, back
by six. Walked his dog at 7:30, 6:15, and 11:30. His job
kept him cooped up over a drafting table.

By Wednesday evening, Morley was ready to move. He
knew Schaeffer would be upset, but he wouldn't wait.
Rudley might be passing the money. He had to be picked
up and scared a little.

Schaeffer argued for the full week that Morley promised after the first drop. "It's only twenty-four hours and it could make a big difference."

Jacobson sided with Schaeffer and Morley finally compromised, arranging for Benson and Jacobson to make the arrest at noon the next day. Schaeffer knew it would set Margaret up as a sitting target, but Morley wouldn't budge.

Margaret woke up early Thursday morning and made herself some coffee. It felt strange sitting down to early morning coffee without her *New York Times*. After so many years the habit had become a ritual. At eight o'clock every morning she had gone to the nearby stationery store to pick up the late edition, but now it would look suspicious to buy the *Times* and then search the cans for a copy later. She missed the daily puzzle.

Why not? she thought, unable to resist. Just this once.

Schaeffer hadn't planned to start his surveillance so early, but when he saw Margaret leave without any bags, he got up and followed her out. She ended up at Riverside Park on one of the benches facing the Hudson. In a few minutes she was engrossed in her paper. Schaeffer chose a bench a block away, stretched out his legs, and settled back to watch some kids throwing a football. In fifteen minutes two more boys joined in, and they soon had a game. The downtown's side scored every time they had the ball. The quarterback threw long accurate passes while the other side had trouble passing and stayed on the ground, running some neat razzle-dazzle. Schaeffer was amused. He was an avid football fan and it was, in miniature, the classic struggle between a great quarterback team and a great running team. He rooted for the downtown team and their budding Namath.

Every now and then he looked toward Margaret. She was still reading her paper.

It was getting near ten and in two hours they'd be busting in on Rudley. Schaeffer groaned and turned back to watch the game. After a few minutes, something broke loose inside his head. It happened slowly at first, but all of a sudden he realized he was looking at something very important. Crucial. He glanced quickly at Margaret again, and then checked his wallet. He had enough for a cab. He left Margaret at the park and took off for the mid-Manhattan public library—to look through microfilm copies of *The New York Times*.

October '75 was in several reels. He was pretty sure it was October. Just enough time for the season to have gotten underway. It was a big month for news, especially on the sports pages. Thirty-five minutes later, a headline jumped out at him: "Lions' Quarterback Dies in Narcotics Overdose."

Schaeffer breezed through the article but stopped in the middle of the last paragraph: ". . . Dennis Rudley's parents, Samuel and Ruth Rudley, were grief-stricken. Friends who are staying with them at their West Seventy-fifth Street apartment . . ."

He made a copy for Morley. It was already 11:15. He'd better call the precinct.

Morley was not at his desk, but Schaeffer left a message demanding he hold up the operation. He took the subway back to the precinct and burst into Morley's office.

"What the hell is this all about?" Morley shouted. "Do you—"

"Where's Jacobson and Benson?" Schaeffer interrupted.

"Outside."

"Here, read this." Schaeffer threw the article in front of Morley. "The *Times*. October 17th, 1975."

Morley read the article through.

Schaeffer plopped himself into the armchair in front of Morley's desk. "A decoy. You know any father would deal in drugs after his son ODed?"

"Shit."

"It's just a hell of a lucky coincidence, that's all. If they had chosen someone else, you'd probably be busting his door down right now, and I'd be right with you."

Morley shouted into the phone, "Get Jacobson and Ben-

son in here right away." He slammed down the receiver.
"You got a good memory, Schaeffer."

"He was a good quarterback. Could have played in the
pro's."

Morley smiled. "Okay, now we got more waiting."

Schaeffer was relieved, but he knew he would have to
keep plugging for Margaret.

"Listen, I don't wanna tell Margaret about the decoy—
the less she knows the better."

Shortly after noon Cotlin called Margaret with instructions for the drop. The mechanics would be different this
time. The pickup was still in a garbage can on the West
Side, but the delivery was to be at the Museum of Natural
History. Margaret was to look for somebody with a
shoulder bag, a *bolsa* with green and orange embroidery.
The money would be wrapped in an identical bag when she
found it. Cotlin told Margaret to wait next to the statue of
Teddy Roosevelt and hand the envelope to the person with
the bolsa. Margaret wondered what she would do if there
were two people with the same bag.

She had just sat down next to Teddy Roosevelt when a
man approached her. His bolsa was identical to hers. He
nodded and sat down, placing his bag in between them.
Margaret carefully slipped the envelope in the open end,
gave the string a tug, and left.

Schaeffer had checked in the air vent after leaving Morley, but by the time he arrived at the museum, Margaret
had already gone. He wasn't worried. She must have
passed their test and it was only a matter of time before
they could make the arrest.

Margaret made five more deliveries, two on Friday, two
on Saturday, and one on Sunday afternoon. They were all
made to different people, but all at the same location,
under the horse in front of the Museum of Natural History.
Schaeffer observed each exchange from a bench across
Central Park West. The contact was always the same type:

young, nicely dressed, and all carrying the same bolsa. Jacobson followed the contacts and photographed them from his van.

Schaeffer had figured on one pickup man, maybe two or three at most, but five didn't make any sense when all the money had to be channeled back again to one top man. It left too much room for error and dishonesty. In their meetings on the bench, Schaeffer always asked Margaret if any of the contacts had spoken to her, if anything they had said might be a further clue, but each time Margaret shook her head. "Nothing. They just pick up the money and walk away. Once someone—the young woman—said thank you. That's all."

An I.D. check revealed that all of Margaret's contacts were students in New York and all were from South America.

Morley called a meeting for Monday afternoon. He hoped that by then he would have enough information to sort things out.

As soon as Schaeffer walked in, he could tell that Morley was onto something. The ashtray was filled with twice the number of butts there normally were.

"So who are we playing with?" Schaeffer asked. "A drug ring or a foreign student loan office?"

"Very funny," Morley growled. "None of them have records in the U.S. The report came in this morning."

Schaeffer picked at his beard with both hands as he paced in front of the desk.

"Come on, come on. You'll burn a hole in the carpet if you walk around in front of my desk anymore. Take a major conviction to get another one."

Schaeffer sat down in front of the desk and stretched out his legs. "Mules," Morley said. "We got a case of runners, I think. All along we figured we were onto a distribution network. Those bags are made in Columbia. All the coke comes from South America. I think what we've got here is a delivery network. Jacobson's done some scouting at the airport. All those kids just flew in from down there."

Schaeffer nodded slowly.

"It seems obvious." Morley rubbed his eyes. "It's about time we get some firsthand information. I want to haul a couple of them in."

"If they still have a tie-in with the operation, you're going to make it hot for Margaret. If they're just couriers then they're out of it. You really want to take that chance?"

"We wait and all we'll get is more names. I don't see any alternative."

"Who you gonna pull in?"

"Nuñez and Ortega." He flipped two pages at him. "You can read up on them. Only I don't want you around when they're in."

Schaeffer glanced at the two reports.

"I'll get Jacobson to bring Nuñez first. When I finish talking to her, we'll do Ortega. I'll let you know if we get anything. Meanwhile, keep a close watch on the old lady."

Rita Nuñez was asleep in her apartment when Jacobson arrived the next morning. A half hour later, she stormed into Morley's office demanding an explanation.

"Sit down please, Miss Nuñez. This may take some time and you're going to get tired standing up."

"What's going to take some time?" She stared at him from the middle of the room.

"Figuring out where you fit into the setup."

"What setup?" she asked.

"We've got photographs of the pickup and we've got a witness. If I sent Sergeant Jacobson back to your apartment I'm sure he'd find the bag they told you to use." He motioned to the chair. "It will be easier for you if you sit down."

She moved to the chair and sank down.

"Now, how did you get into this thing?" There was silence for a moment. Morley waited.

"Am I under arrest?"

"No, Miss Nuñez. We just want to clarify a few things."

"Then you won't mind if I call a lawyer."

Morley pounded his fist on the desk. "Yes, I do mind, goddamn it. You call a lawyer and I'll put you under arrest.

Then I'll contact Immigration and let them have a go at you. Listen, you tell me what I want to know and you can get up and walk out. If you start pulling shit on me, you can forget about your U.S. diploma." He leaned back. "Now, what's it gonna be?"

She looked out the window again and sighed. "It was a stupid idea to begin with. I don't know why the hell I ever fell for it."

As Morley suspected, she was only a minor cog in the operation. But what she had told him was enough to put him in motion. He had been on the right track. They were mules, but he wanted confirmation from Ortega.

His story was essentially the same as Rita Nuñez's. He began by describing his meeting with an old school friend in Bogotá, a boy who had dropped out in his last year of school because he liked expensive things and couldn't wait.

"He took me to meet some of his new friends. They were much older, and I didn't feel very comfortable with them. But after a few drinks we got to talking and one of them asked me if I wanted to make some easy money. I was coming to New York and I knew it would be expensive."

"Cocaine?"

The boy nodded. "Two keys."

"How'd you get it in?"

"On an airplane."

Morley looked impatient. "I know you flew here. I asked you how you got the drugs through customs."

Ortega leaned forward. "On the airplane, like I said. There is this one flight direct to New York from Caracas that continues on to Washington. I hid the drugs in the bathroom—in dummy rolls of toilet paper which I carried with me. I cleared customs in New York and then reboarded the same plane to Washington. There are no customs on domestic flights, so I simply got off the plane and took the shuttle back to New York with the cocaine."

Morley looked over at Jacobson. "Don't they check that?"

Jacobson shrugged. "What, cut each roll of toilet paper in half?"

Morley shook his head and turned back to Ortega. "Then what?"

"I'd get paid only after I delivered the stuff in New York. They said I'd be contacted after I arrived, and after two days in New York I got a note at school. Any Monday I wanted I could just drop the stuff, wrapped up in a yellow plastic bag, into a certain garbage can at 9 A.M."

"Where was this particular can?"

"In Queens, Thirty-fourth and Astoria Boulevard, next to the supermarket."

"And how were you going to get paid after you dropped the stuff off?"

"In Bogotá they gave me this shoulder bag and told me it would establish contact with the people who were to pay me. They were supposed to call me and tell me where and when I should be waiting for the money. When I dropped the stuff off I was supposed to put my telephone number inside. The guys in Bogotá told me it would take a week or so to get paid since all the stuff was tested up here for purity."

"Ortega," Morley said, getting up, "you may be the most naïve kid I've ever met. Christ. You risk the two flights, customs, and a pickup, and you have no guarantees. Two keys are worth close to a hundred and fifty thousand on the street. They could have stiffed you."

"Oh, no. You see I was to make two drops in Queens. I'd only do the second one after I got paid for the first. If I wasn't paid, then I could get rid of the second kilo myself." He leaned back. "I wasn't worried at all. After the first drop, I'd already have a thousand dollars. You know, it was all worked out. Besides, they knew I'd be making at least two trips a year for the next four years. Why spoil a good thing?"

"Is it possible for you to get in touch with the New York agents again?"

"I guess so. I'd just have to put something, maybe some

powder, in a yellow plastic bag with a note in it and drop it in the same can at the right time."

"Okay. That's all for now."

Morley booted Ortega out with a warning that someone would be watching the can at all times, and if he went anywhere near it, he'd be on the next plane to Bogotá. A few minutes later Morley filled Schaeffer in on the interviews.

"Next Monday, take a day off from Margaret. Try your luck at Astoria Boulevard. I want you there by eight."

"What about . . . ?"

"Don't worry. I'll put someone else on her for the day."

"Thanks, Mac. Why me?"

Morley got serious. "Look, you got a special interest in this thing, and if we want Margaret off the hook, we've got to do this right. I don't want to give immunity to every goddamned student that's involved in this thing."

"Right." Schaeffer got up and walked toward the door. "I wonder why they don't drop the stuff off in Manhattan. Seems they could use the same network they've set up here. Funny . . ."

# Seven

SCHAEFFER WOULD HAVE LIKED AN extra hour between the sheets. "I need a rest," he told Jacobson as they walked west on Astoria Boulevard. "It's a typical Monday. I feel like I'm dragging a drunk around, and every now and then I realize it's me."

Jacobson was wearing jeans and carrying a shopping bag full of flowers wrapped in small bouquets.

"A fine pair we make."

"Authenticity is what we're after," Jacobson replied. "Bums are supposed to look tired."

"Yeah, and that's enough with the postgraduate routine. There's the can." He nodded across the street. "See you later."

Jacobson sauntered across the street, walked past the garbage can, and kept going for about fifty yards. He sat down on one of the stoops, put the bag next to him, and opened for business. He hawked his flowers now and then but was careful not to interest too many people.

Schaeffer settled himself in a coffee shop halfway down the block. From his seat by the window he had a clear view of the can about thirty yards away. He ordered a coffee, opened a copy of *The News*, and waited. It was 8:05.

By 8:30 the streets began to fill. Schaeffer watched the flow of people, ignoring the paper. He knew nothing would happen until after nine, but he was trying to spot someone who might be waiting for a pickup. He kept an eye on the can, but as far as he could tell, most of the trash being dumped consisted of morning newspapers and empty coffee containers. Every can in the city must be getting the same kind of trash. At noon it would change from newspapers to sandwich wrappers and later on to the discarded bags of afternoon shoppers. He envisioned the thousands of cans with the same distinct levels, like watermarks in the city's daily life cycle. Christ, he thought, this job is really getting to me.

He scanned the street once more to take his mind off the tons of stratified city garbage. About twenty feet away an older woman was leaning against a street sign, rummaging in an old, scuffed-up pocketbook. She fitted the part. Her clothes matched the pocketbook, and she didn't seem to be going anywhere. He glanced up the street at Jacobson, who was also watching her. She kept reaching in her bag, as though she was searching for something. Finally she pulled her hand out and walked to the corner. Schaeffer looked at his watch: 8:45. She was a little early. A bus came and left. The woman was gone.

"Shit," Schaeffer murmured. He hadn't even noticed it was a bus stop.

By 9:45 Schaeffer was on his third cup of coffee and was getting uneasy stares from the waiter. The traffic on the sidewalk had thinned out and every now and then someone would walk past the can and throw in a gum wrapper or empty pack of cigarettes. But nothing in a yellow plastic bag.

Schaeffer paid and was walking out to speak with Jacobson when a city garbage truck made a turn on to Astoria Boulevard two blocks away. He watched as it made the two pickups farther down the avenue and then dumped the meager contents of their staked-out can. Schaeffer walked toward Jacobson as the truck moved on to the next block.

"I think it's blown for the day. No one came and no one's going to come." He looked up to find the truck and just caught sight of its tail end as it rounded the corner two blocks away. "Unless . . ."

"Unless what?"

Schaeffer exploded. "Jesus, we just saw the pickup."

Jacobson turned around to look.

"Come on, man. The truck! Did you get the number?"

Schaeffer picked up Jacobson's flowers and started running down the street, with Jacobson following close behind.

"Truck number 84 5DP 56."

Morley stopped pacing but his hands were flying in all directions. "But that's its job. That's what we pay taxes for, so city garbage trucks can pick up city garbage from city garbage cans. Jesus! Why don't you just tell me whoever picked up the stuff gave you the slip."

"Because no one came near the can between 8:05 and 9:45 when the truck empties it. Isn't that right, Jake?"

Jacobson nodded.

"A goddamned garbage truck! I'm open to reason, but just tell me how the hell you arrived at this amazing bit of detection. Christ almighty, if this gets out, there's going to be one hell of a reaction from downtown." Morley threw himself into his desk chair and waited, his arms folded tightly against his chest.

Schaeffer shuffled over to one of the windows and looked out into the street. "First of all, as I told you, no one came. If Nuñez and Ortega were straight with us, there was a possible delivery this morning. And unless they pointed us to the wrong can, the stash would have been lost. That's one point. Then, I was wondering why Queens when there's already a pickup system here on the West Side. Why get another person involved when it isn't necessary? That seemed stupid to me, but then I saw it. It's because they had a totally different system for the dope. There was no way they wanted to risk the stuff being hauled away by mistake. So they had to haul it off on purpose. By using a garbage truck it would be easy to see if there had been a drop when they dumped the can. A yellow plastic bag, it would be obvious. So they had two choices. They could either pick it out and stash it in the cab, or let it go in and deal with it later. I think they left the stuff with the rest of the trash in case they ran into trouble. That avoids the second problem. After all, they're not responsible for all the crap that's in the truck."

"Seems like it would make things a lot harder for them finding it later."

"Have you ever spent any time studying the type of garbage that's thrown in those cans?"

"No, I never had that pleasure."

"Well, it's not yellow plastic bags. If I'm right, I'm sure that can was chosen for a reason. It's probably one of the first on the route. If you check, I'll bet truck 84 5DP 56 starts on Astoria Boulevard and Thirty-second Street where I saw it round the corner."

"So?"

"Well, if there was a drop they would probably do a few more cans, stop to make a call, and drive to a nearby point where they could transfer the stuff. Very simple. Only today they didn't have a drop, so they went to work on an apartment building."

"You realize," Morley said, "what you're telling me is pure speculation. You didn't see anything this morning."

"That's right . . . pure mind power." Schaeffer leaned back.

Morley hesitated. "You know, if you weren't so arrogant . . ." He fished out two paper clips from a cup on his desk. "Jacobson?"

Jacobson looked over at Schaeffer. "The whole crew would have to be in on it."

"So, they probably lay out several thousand dollars a year for the service," Schaeffer said. "We're talking about an operation that must do millions. If I were the boss, I wouldn't hesitate paying that amount just for the extra insurance."

Morley was fidgeting with the paper clips. The room was silent for a few moments. Morley threw the clips into the wastebasket. "Hired scavengers, decoys, foreign students, Colombian shoulder bags, and now bribing the city's garbagemen. Jesus."

"Truck number 84 5DP 56."

"Yeah, yeah. I got it. Schaeffer, find out about the bastards on that truck."

When Schaeffer left, Morley turned to Jacobson. "We're gonna need a couple of pounds of sugar. See if you can scare some up."

# Eight

"WHAT DO YOU MEAN LONGLEY DIDN'T get anything?" Daker was furious.

Cotlin raised his shoulders in a shrug. "That's what he told me."

Daker shook his head. He picked up a pencil and tapped it on the desk top. "You think Longley's on the level?" He had assumed "Doc" Longley would no sooner grab a shipment than he would a snort. He was a graduate chemist with a bent for the slightly illegal use of his talents. He had set up the entire lab procedure, as well as the delivery schedule.

"Longley's straight," Cotlin said. "He knows we can always check it out with Matthews."

"Sure, sure," Daker said. "And Matthews?"

Cotlin was sure Daker knew, but he went through the routine anyway. "He's got two other guys on the truck. If he pulled a fast one the other two gotta be in on it. I don't think they're up to it." Daker nodded, and Cotlin tried to think of something else to ease Daker's mood. Daker often got like this when things didn't happen on the button. "What about that letter from Colombia—something about it being hard to find mules?"

"They said it was slow, not dead. But that letter came a month ago."

"Well, maybe it's just coming out now. You know how those students are. They meet a girl on the way, decide to shack up for an extra week. Happens all the time. I know I . . ."

"What about Binton?" Daker interrupted.

"Come on, Max. You know she doesn't enter into that end. She doesn't get anywhere near it." Jesus, Cotlin thought, this guy . . .

"I know," Daker said. "Just curious. It's the first time in three months nothing came into the lab. Mund still keeping an eye on her?"

"Yeah. How long you want to keep that up?" Cotlin sounded impatient. Daker had hit his sore spot.

"I'll let you know." Daker reached for the newspaper hanging off one end of his desk, picked up a pencil, and bit down on the rubber end. He slapped the paper over on its back and bent over the day's crossword puzzle.

Cotlin knew it was time to go. Daker wouldn't talk to anybody for the next half hour.

"What the hell is an Eskimo boat in five letters?"

"Umiak," Margaret said and smiled to herself. Sunlight streamed into her apartment and warmed her face. Whenever she got one across right away it turned out to be an omen. Tuesday morning she had been stumped by "Arabian garment," which turned out to be "djellaba." It had rained all day.

"And one down is ukase." Margaret looked over at the phone and wondered if it would ring. It had been two days since the last call. She was getting impatient. She got tired of waiting for Cotlin's call, wondering if each day would be her last on the job, wondering when she could get back into her old clothes and see her friends again. It was all well and good to try to help out, but six weeks had gone by and she wondered if she was really helping at all. She had only a vague idea of what the police were doing since she was able to exchange only a few abrupt words with Schaeffer whenever she saw him. Margaret had never kept this silent in her life. Certainly Cotlin was no great conversationalist.

One o'clock came and went. No one had called all morning. Margaret finally went out, leaving Schaeffer a note to meet her at their bench, and took a slow walk down the street, her bags in tow.

When Schaeffer showed up Margaret cleared her throat and spilled out all her complaints, hinting that she wanted to quit.

He had been expecting it but it would be dangerous for her to quit now. The organization would have to silence her for their own safety. Regardless of the fact that she had done all she could for the police, and that her job was essentially over, she had to continue in her role until they got the case wrapped up.

It wasn't an easy thing to tell her.

Margaret looked skeptically at Schaeffer and smiled. "Well, I trust you," she said. "Only I wish you'd hurry up. Last week I cut my hand fishing for their silly money." She held up her hand for him to see but remembered they were in the middle of Broadway, in view of everyone. She continued the gesture and straightened her hair. "Oh, well, I've enjoyed our little chat," she sighed. "It's better when you let me know what's happening. Makes me feel useful. But not too much longer, huh?"

"I'll get in touch as soon as something else develops. Take care of your hand." He got up and crossed the avenue. Margaret watched him go, thinking that maybe "umiak" and "Koran" were wrong although she couldn't understand it. "Aardvark" fit so nicely.

Mund waited until Margaret left the bench. His surveillance was always uneventful but this time he sensed that Margaret wasn't as innocent as she looked. He watched Schaeffer walk down Broadway.

Mund had watched the two of them talking together on the bench. It was almost as though they weren't talking with each other, but to a third person. Strange. It was unlike her. He had seen her get involved in a discussion before, and it was always a close and intimate, even physical, exchange. With this guy it was aloof and almost secretive, like the way she had showed her hand to him. He had seen her momentary hesitation and awkward recovery. Could be some poor slob she had befriended, could be just some bum, but he'd better check.

Mund followed Schaeffer. The guy walks like an athlete, smooth and brisk, not like a regular wino.

Schaeffer stopped at a newsstand and glanced at the headlines, then eyed one of the phone booths at the corner and walked over slowly while scrounging in his pockets for a quarter. Nothing much to report, but they might need him back at the office. He got Morley and briefly filled him in on his talk with Margaret.

Mund walked up behind Schaeffer and leaned against a nearby car pretending to wait for the phone. He strained to hear Schaeffer's conversation, but Schaeffer had felt his approach and, moved by a sense of caution, turned around and smiled. He gestured he'd only be a minute and continued to talk to Morley.

"That's right, two on Adam's Baby in the third."

He hung up and moved down the block before looking back. The man who had been waiting was just dropping in his dime. What the hell, Schaeffer thought. Can't be too careful.

Mund finally got Daker on the phone. "I'll tell you about it later. See if there's a horse called Adam's Baby running today. If there isn't, I might have something."

Schaeffer walked into Morley's office an hour later. "You think this is a branch of Off Track Betting or something? Christ, almighty."

Schaeffer grinned at him. "Just being careful—eavesdroppers. It wouldn't hurt to put a couple of bucks on Adam's Baby, though. The jockey's kid brother's a friend of mine."

"Very funny."

Schaeffer winced at the yellow plastic bag and the several boxes of sugar on Morley's desk.

"So, you're really climbing the wall. Can't take long until they get a real drop. Shit, they get anywhere near this and they'll go straight for Margaret."

"No . . . they won't. They'll think one of their couriers got greedy. She doesn't get anywhere near the coke. And they know that—they planned it that way. We're going to make the drop and we'll watch them pick it up. In a couple of hours we'll have the warrant and we can bust them. Two hours, tops. They may not even test the stuff for a day, maybe two, so whatever we use it doesn't matter. We just can't wait any longer."

"At least you could have gotten some real stuff from the property clerk."

Morley shook his head. "Not after the French thing. Best I can do is to hold the drop until the truck starts up Astoria. If anybody makes a drop beforehand, we'll hold off. How's that? If you're so sure there's going to be another drop, that ought to make you feel better."

Small consolation, Schaeffer thought. And if there wasn't another, they would get to this bag right away. Six weeks of work and we come up with a big zero. He pulled out one of Morley's cigarettes.

"We'll have six men on it, you included."

"Jacobson?"

"Yeah. Flowers and all. We got the TV van and a couple of plain wheels."

Morley pulled out a cigarette for himself. "As soon as we find where the stuff is going, we get somebody downtown with the warrant. Then it's just a matter of traffic. We bust in and pick up anything around. There's got to be a connecting link to the upstairs. If they try to move out before we get there, we got a six-man tail."

"So, what're you doin' with Margaret then? You leavin' her to those dogs? Some nice life she's got from now on. Here she thought she was helping us."

"Schaeffer, Jacobson and the rest agreed. It's getting more dangerous to wait around. Meanwhile more and more stuff is hitting the street. Look, she should have known what was in the cards when she signed on with us. Nothin's gonna go wrong."

"Yeah, well, I don't like the odds."

"Cool out, Schaeffer." Morley blew out his last mouthful of smoke and mashed the cigarette into the ashtray. "Don't worry. I know what I'm doing."

# Nine

FOUR PLAINCLOTHESMEN WERE POSI-
tioned near the can on Astoria Boulevard by 8:30 Monday
morning. Morley was at the wheel of an unmarked car
parked midway down the block. Inspector Robbins, the
head of the narcotics division, sat next to him, sipping
coffee. A package about the size of a small loaf of bread,
covered in yellow plastic and bound twice across with
masking tape, was on the seat between them. It weighed
exactly one kilo.

Schaeffer was in the coffee shop. Jacobson was selling
flowers on the stoop. Staunton was parked in a black Ford
at the end of the bus stop, and Benson was across the street
in the radio-TV repair van, ready to get Jacobson when the
garbage truck took off.

Morley kept his eye on the can to see if any other drops
were going in, occasionally glancing over at Schaeffer,
who was fifteen feet away.

By 9:15 nothing had changed.

9:25. Morley adjusted the rearview mirror and began to
watch the street behind him. Once the garbage truck made
the turn, he figured he had about four minutes, plenty of
time to get out, walk the half block, and make the drop.
Robbins also had his eyes glued to the sideview mirror,
waiting for the first signs of the countdown.

What the hell is going wrong? Schaeffer thought. Two Mondays in a row . . . He looked at his watch. 9:30.

When he looked up, Morley was just getting out of the car, package in hand. Turning farther, he saw the garbage truck slowing to a stop two blocks away. Shit, he thought, it's going to happen.

Morley slowly walked past Schaeffer's window, gave him a helpless look, and continued toward the can. Schaeffer watched resignedly.

Out of the corner of his eye Schaeffer saw a taxi pull up at the end of the block. He felt weak as the cab door opened and the passenger leaped out. He was a short young man wearing a madras jacket. He was carrying a yellow plastic bag.

Schaeffer started to get up, but there was nothing he could do—Morley was already halfway across the street. If only Morley would turn around. In seconds Morley had made the drop and was on his way back to the car.

Morley's face dropped when he saw the man, but they passed each other in silence.

Schaeffer was on the street in time to see the man get into another cab. The garbage truck was already crawling toward them, only a block away.

As the truck stopped, two men jumped from their perches and dragged the can to the back end. Schaeffer sauntered by to get a better look. Three yellow plastic packages tumbled into the hatchway. He cursed softly to himself. Someone must have made a drop before 8:30.

Close to $300,000 worth of drugs and they don't even bat an eyelash, Schaeffer thought. As the truck pulled away he saw the number and nodded at Morley. Schaeffer got into the Ford next to Staunton as Morley and Robbins drove by and then leaned back into the seat and rubbed his eyes. He felt Staunton shift into gear and pull out. The TV van followed close behind.

The garbage truck passed the turnoff it had taken the previous week and continued down the boulevard. Morley stayed about one hundred feet behind.

After a few turns the area changed from partly residential to mostly small, one-story factory buildings, and the traffic thinned.

Schaeffer felt pretty certain that the garbage men were still unaware they were being followed. When the truck made a right turn, Staunton braked to the curb and allowed the TV repair van to pass. Schaeffer flicked on his radio. There was a loud crackle before Jacobson's voice came through.

"Two blocks down Twelfth Street, pulling into driveway next to number sixty-seven. One man getting out. We're going to pass."

As Schaeffer and Staunton got out of their car, Robbins and Morley pulled up behind them. The radio crackled again.

"Stopped thirty yards away. Building has a sign in front. Hydrocryogenics Laboratory. Repeat. H-Y-D-R-O-C-R-Y-O-G-E-N-I-C-S."

Morley, Schaeffer, and Staunton started toward the building, leaving Robbins behind to radio headquarters.

The street was littered with broken glass and uncollected trash. The garbage truck idled next to a one-story cinderblock building about forty feet wide.

Schaeffer flattened himself against the side of a building across the street. One of the garbage men was reaching into the back of the truck while the other glanced nervously up and down the street. Another man in a white coat came out of the building, grabbed the three yellow packages, and then disappeared inside. The truck drove away.

Schaeffer watched Morley walk by the entrance and turn the corner at the end of the block. They had the street boxed in. Ten o'clock. He pulled out his pack of cigarettes and settled down to wait for the warrant.

At 10:30 Daker received a frantic phone call.

"Wait a minute," he interrupted. "Say it again. A key of *sugar*?"

"Pure cane. The other two were okay."

Daker leaned back in his chair.

"It's the first time it's happened," the voice continued. "I thought you'd like to know right away."

"Is there a note inside, an address, anything?"

"No, nothing. The other two were Martinez and Valente."

"Hold on a minute." Daker reached into his top drawer and pulled out a folder. He checked off the two names and glanced at the rest of the list. There were five left, but three had picked up no more than a week before.

"Okay, thanks, Longley. Just keep the stuff there. I'll send someone over to pick it up."

"Sorry."

Daker hesitated. "So am I."

Daker looked out the window for several minutes, then turned to his desk, scribbled a note, and stuffed it into an envelope. He pushed the buzzer and asked Cotlin to come in.

"Listen," he said. "Something's come up. I want you to find Mund right away. Give him this. He'll understand. You know where he is?"

"Yeah, I think so. What's the rush?"

"I said right away." Daker slammed his fist on the table and sank back into his chair.


Schaeffer crushed out his eighth cigarette. 11:30. Nothing had happened. Occasionally he caught a glimpse of Morley looking around the corner. A few cars and a few pedestrians had gone by but none had stopped.

Schaeffer thought about Margaret constantly. Today she'd be alone, without a cover. It made him uneasy. If only they'd hurry with the warrant.

A taxicab rounded the corner and stopped in front of Hydrocryogenics. Schaeffer leaned closer to the building and motioned Staunton across the street. A man got out of the cab and walked to the front door. When he turned around to look down the street, Schaeffer caught sight of his face. He had seen it before, somewhere recently, but he couldn't place it. The cab stayed while the man disappeared into the building. Apparently he was intending to stay only a short time.

Five minutes passed. Ten. The cab driver got out and looked into one of the windows. He shrugged and tried the front door, but it was locked. He went back and leaned against the side of his cab. Suddenly Schaeffer remembered the man at the phone booth, slouching against one of the cars waiting to make a call. His heart raced. They must suspect Margaret already.

He heard footsteps and whirled around to see Robbins and a uniformed policeman running toward him. Robbins waved the paper, but Schaeffer was already on the street. Staunton was behind him and Jacobson and Benson were getting out of the truck. Schaeffer went directly to the side door. It was locked. He knocked, pulled out his revolver, and held it ready. A few seconds went by.

"Fuck 'em," he said, firing two .38 slugs into the lock and kicking the door open. Robbins was right behind him, and the two men peered inside. Nothing moved.

Several tables held laboratory equipment but there were few places anyone could hide. Robbins went to open the front door while Schaeffer checked the bathroom. He walked over to the glassed-in office. A window opened to the rear behind the large desk.

"We're too late," he said as Morley walked up to him. He pointed in the direction of the bloodstained white coat.

Robbins followed Schaeffer and Morley into the office. The dead man had his knees pulled up to his chest, one hand pressed to his cheek. A thin line of blood trickled through his fingers.

"Might as well check the place anyway," Morley said, pointing toward the office. The files in the drawer had been rifled. "I'll get the print men down here, but I don't think we're going to get a goddamned thing."

As Morley looked at the body in the white coat he knew they had arrived at the end. It was more than likely that in killing the lab technician the top level had eliminated all connections to itself.

The taxi driver was waiting by the side door. After a

few minutes of questioning, Morley took his number and let him go. The passenger had come from Eightieth and Broadway in Manhattan, right around the corner from Margaret.

"Let's go," Morley said to Schaeffer as they walked out of the glass office. "We got a date with three garbage men."

"No, that can wait," Schaeffer said, heading for the front door. "I'm going after Margaret. She's next."

Morley put a hand on his shoulder and tried to slow him down. "Wait a minute," he said.

"I recognized the guy that got out of the taxi, the one that pulled this number. He followed me last week."

Morley nodded at him. "Take Jacobson with you. You'd better hurry."

# Ten

MARGARET WAITED FOR HER MORNING
call. It didn't come and she left at eleven. She had almost
become careless and had even shed some of her costume.
She checked the can at Eighty-seventh and West End but
there was no message from Schaeffer.

The bench at Eightieth Street was already full of people
sunning themselves beneath the warm morning sun and the
cloudless sky. Some were strangers, mere transients, unlike
her friends whom she could always count on to be in a
certain spot at a certain time. Like Sid, with his mono-
logues on the latest from Aqueduct and his endless free
advice. Or Bertie with her bag of bread crumbs. Or even
Roosa "the old juicer" who used the benches to sleep off
his hangovers and only joined the conversations when the
subject turned to bars. Margaret thought it was too bad
everyone didn't have such good friends. She settled next to
Bertie as gently as possible so as not to disturb the cluster
of pigeons that had gathered around for their daily handout.
Bertie smiled at Margaret and pointed to one of the birds.

"Sick. Can you see it? Poor thing's not eating enough."

Margaret looked at the scrawny bird and smiled. "The
way you feed them, Bertie, I'm surprised they all don't
have gout."

Bertie dipped into the bag and dashed a handful of

crumbs onto the sidewalk. She held another handful out to the thin bird. It came over, pecked at the bread once or twice, and walked away.

"He's been like that for four days. Haven't seen you in quite a while, Margaret. I told Sid you mustn't be feeling too well."

"Oh, I'm all right," Margaret replied. "Just a little busy, that's all." She moved over to make a space on the bench when she saw Sid come over. To Bertie's annoyance, he made no effort to avoid the cluster of birds and walked right through them.

"Hullo," Sid said.

Bertie ignored him and turned toward Margaret, but Sid didn't seem to notice that Bertie was upset. He launched into the story of his killing on a long-shot daily double at the O.T.B. Margaret had become used to Sid's stories over the past seven years and figured that if only 10 percent of them were true he could easily buy an apartment on Park Avenue. Sid pulled out the daily racing form and began making notes while Margaret and Bertie chatted.

"My elevator is on the blink," Margaret said. "It's the second time in two months, and it'll be out of service from noon to midnight."

"What will you do?" Bertie asked. "You can't walk up ten flights."

"What else can I do, Bertie, sleep here on the bench?"

"Well, I won't let you do it." She brushed the few remaining crumbs from her skirt. "Ten flights. Why, you'd be out cold before you reached the seventh floor. Listen, I've got a couch in my place. You can spend the night with me. I never have company and it would be fun."

Margaret protested but Bertie insisted.

"I have to be home tomorrow by ten o'clock," Margaret said.

"Yes, of course." Bertie looked at her watch. "We should hurry over to your place to get some things for you."

Forty minutes later Schaeffer and Jacobson pulled up to Margaret's building in an unmarked car. He had already cruised down Broadway but had failed to spot her. The elevator man told Schaeffer he had seen Margaret leave about a half hour earlier with a suitcase. She'd had a friend with her.

"Will you be on tomorrow morning?" Schaeffer asked the attendant.

"I go on at seven-thirty. What ya got?"

Schaeffer handed him a ten dollar bill and showed him his I.D. "Call me at this number when she comes in. It's very important."

"She in some kinda trouble?" he asked.

"Not if you call me," Schaeffer said as he turned to walk out.

Schaeffer bought a copy of *Psychology Today* on his way back to the precinct. Page twelve had a narrow margin but he managed to squeeze in his message.

M. COME TO SEE ME <u>IMMEDIATELY</u>. PUT MAGAZINE BACK AND WALK <u>DIRECTLY</u> TO OUR OFFICE. URGENT.

S.

Schaeffer rolled up the magazine and stuck it in his back pocket. He would drop it in their message can the next morning. If the elevator man missed her, she was sure to get the message when she began her rounds.

# Eleven

DAKER HAD BEEN ON THE PHONE TO South America since Cotlin left the office to find Mund.

Cotlin was back in an hour. He didn't know what was in the note he had just delivered, but he knew it must have been important from the look Mund had given him. Daker filled him in on what was happening and on how he was trying to rearrange the operation.

"Those garbage men can't touch us, can they?" Cotlin interrupted.

"No. Whatever they know goes no further than Longley, and by now Mund will have taken care of that. There's no way to trace us."

"That's good," Cotlin breathed.

Daker continued his discussion about re-establishing a functioning network. It wouldn't be too difficult. The ground rules were laid down. They would need some slightly different tactics. He had arranged a temporary halt to the couriers.

Mund walked in at 12:30, carrying a large paper bag and a folder wedged inside a newspaper. He opened the bag, spilled three yellow parcels onto the desk, and put the folder from Longley's file next to them. "Lab analysis for purity, RG 273 thru 548 . . . Mr. Daker" was written across the top.

"Thorough, wasn't he?" Cotlin said as he glanced at the long columns of neat figures.

"He was." Mund smirked.

"Did you get everything?" Daker asked, looking up from the papers.

"Yeah."

"Problems?"

"No . . . only I caught a glimpse of the guy that's always with the old lady, the guy I told you about. He was waiting around the corner from Longley's place. I knew he was a cop."

Daker slammed his fist on the desk and looked over to Cotlin. "So, it looks like I have one more expendable employee." He slowly got up from his desk and opened the wall safe. He was careful to keep his back to Cotlin and Mund. "A present from the 'Doc,'" he said, turning around and holding out a small box about the size of a pack of cigarettes. "One of his earlier projects."

"You want me to handle it?" Cotlin asked.

"Can you?" Daker asked sarcastically.

Cotlin nodded. "I know how it works," he said, staring at the box.

"Early tomorrow morning."

Cotlin gently fingered the lid. "Don't worry, you'll read about it in the evening papers."

Daker looked down at the three yellow packages. They all looked alike. He opened the nearest one, dipped in a finger, and touched it to his tongue. "Bunch of fools. Too cheap to use the real thing." He pushed the two other bags across the desk to Cotlin. "Take these two and distribute them right away. Hold on to the other one."

# Twelve

MARGARET AND BERTIE SAW A MOVIE at the RKO and shopped for dinner afterward. Margaret had never been to Bertie's house and over pot roast she talked about her husband, Oscar, and the meals they used to make together.

"Funny how little things like smells and melodies can set you back so distinctly," she said, "even more so than pictures and letters." She stopped and breathed in deeply, closing her eyes as she did so.

Bertie chuckled. "It's the same for me, only it's spaghetti and meatballs. Tony used to love my spaghetti. I'm glad you're here to share a meal with me. Who wants to cook for an hour and a half if there's no one but you to eat it?"

Margaret nodded.

They lingered over coffee until they both decided that they were tired from such a full day.

Margaret slept easily on the strange couch, dreaming of Oscar and days at Coney Island until she felt herself being gently shaken. Bertie was leaning over her and bright light streamed in through the lace-curtained windows. She smelled the faint aroma of freshly made coffee.

"My but you were sleeping soundly," Bertie said, putting a hand to her cheek.

"Must have been out like a light. I usually don't sleep too well in strange places. Oscar always used to fall asleep before me when we were traveling. Then he'd start snoring and I'd be up half the night with the pillow over my head."

Over a breakfast of buttered toast, marmalade, and coffee, they discussed old times. Bertie could remember eggs at eighteen cents a dozen, but Margaret surprised her. She went as far back as milk at fifteen cents a quart.

There was a loud thud outside the front door.

Bertie jumped up. "Surprise for you," she said, going to the door and reappearing with a copy of *The New York Times*. "The nice young man from 5C. He goes to work at nine and leaves me his copy."

She handed the paper to Margaret. "Why don't you read a little while I straighten up the dishes and things?" Margaret made a move to help but Bertie insisted she stay put.

Margaret read the front page and the obituaries before turning to the crossword. She couldn't resist the lure of the clean white boxes and, to her surprise, after fifteen minutes she had completed all but the bottom right corner.

"Say, Bertie, what's a word for jeweler's polishing compound?"

"Only thing I know is Brasso," Bertie said. "Never needed anything else."

"Doesn't fit," Margaret murmured. "But I guess I'll never find out. We'd better go." She put the paper down reluctantly, pushed herself to her feet, and took Bertie's arm.

They walked south on Broadway and stopped occasionally to look in some of the windows, trying to make the trip as long as possible. They promised to spend another evening together soon, and then each went her separate way.

The elevator had been fixed and the elevator man nodded hello as Margaret entered the car. He debated whether or not to mention his meeting with Schaeffer, but decided he had better not interfere. He would phone the number Schaeffer had given him as soon as he went on his coffee break.

Margaret heard her phone ringing as she got out of the

elevator. She knew she was late and rushed to her door but had trouble finding her keys. She stumbled nervously into the apartment, dropping her things, and then cautiously picked up the receiver.

"Where've you been, hey? I've been calling you since ten. You're supposed to be around."

Margaret sat down. She had almost forgotten about who she was supposed to be. "Sorry. I went out to the store." She tried to give her voice an air of innocence, and the voice on the other end seemed to calm down a bit. "Well, at least I got hold of you. We got a very important pickup. Big rush. How long will it take you to get up to Ninetieth and Columbus?"

"You mean right now?"

"Right. Soon as I hang up."

"But I always . . ."

"Never mind that. This is special."

"Well, I guess about fifteen minutes."

"Come on, I know the area. Shouldn't take more than ten."

Margaret shrugged. "Okay, ten."

Margaret took down all the information. The money was in a cigar box this time, the lid had been taped down, and the box would be inside an old shirt.

"We're using small bills now," the voice said, "that's why the box. But you can open it and take yours out."

Margaret banged down the phone. She thought it was strange they were in such a rush and she was tired of having her life interrupted. She had wanted to spend some time cleaning her apartment but at least she wouldn't have to make a detour to check Schaeffer's can. She would pass right near it.

Rose moved slowly up the street, her bags still only half full from her morning's tour. She breathed with difficulty and stopped at the corner of Eighty-seventh Street to rest for a moment. She eased her shopping bags to the sidewalk and fumbled in a nearby can for several seconds. The glossy edge of a magazine caught her eye and she lifted it out to study the cover. She had never found one like it before. Her mouth tried to form the words as she looked at the picture of the young child on the cover . . . *Psychology Today*. She slowly flipped through but it didn't look all that good. The articles were too long and there weren't many pictures, but she decided there were enough, and she stuffed the magazine into one of her bags.

If she had turned around, she might have seen Margaret walking three blocks behind her, making her way toward the same can.

Schaeffer rushed to Margaret's building the minute the elevator man called, but the man had no idea where she had gone and she hadn't left a note in the air vent. He ran out of the building and toward their message can on West End Avenue.

When he got there, Margaret was nowhere in sight.

There were a few crumpled scraps in the can, but no magazine. He stepped back a few paces to check the street corner and to make sure he'd left his message in the right place. He wasn't sure of anything anymore, but Sanitation had assured him that they emptied the can early in the morning, before his drop. And, even if Margaret had picked out the magazine, her instructions were to put it back.

He wondered if he had been followed, if his pursuers had fished it out after he had left it off. He called Morley from a phone booth a few yards away, but Margaret hadn't turned up at the precinct either. They decided they would cruise the area, Jacobson and Schaeffer in one car and Morley and Staunton in another. It was the only choice they had left.

Margaret had checked the can but had found nothing from Schaeffer. She was a little behind schedule but figured that a few minutes here or there didn't matter. She had to walk slowly because of the weight of her bags. She had filled them with a Sunday *Times* two weeks ago, so they wouldn't flutter in the wind, but it was a weight she didn't need and she stopped at a can on the next corner and threw out the heavy load.

She was about to continue on her route when her eye caught the edge of another paper. It was open to the crossword, and as she looked closer she felt a little tremor of excitement. It was the puzzle she hadn't had time to finish that morning and whoever had thrown it away had only finished a quarter of it. The penciled-in words were scattered randomly throughout the puzzle and no attempt had been made to follow through and connect them. One of the penciled-in words was fifty across . . . "tripoli." Margaret beamed.

"Jeweler's compound . . . tripoli." She quickly picked up her bags and walked a few feet to the steps of a church where she sat down with the paper in her lap and started searching for a pencil in the bag closest to her.

Morley and Schaeffer were covering the area block by block. They had agreed that Eighty-sixth Street would be the cut-off point. Anything north was Schaeffer's, anything south, Morley's. Several times Schaeffer offered Jacobson to slow down while he peered more closely at someone who resembled Margaret, but each time it turned out to be a stranger. They were covering the side streets back and forth between Central Park West and Riverside Drive. They could catch the avenues later. Schaeffer leaned forward, his eyes darting from one side of the street to the other. They accelerated on the empty blocks and used the siren whenever they could to save time.

They sped past Margaret on Ninetieth Street. She heard the siren, but didn't look up. She was bent over the paper concentrating on the last word in the puzzle.

When she had finished, she got up and flipped the paper back into the can. Thirty-five minutes had passed since she had gotten the call, but she felt satisfied and thought it a worthwhile delay.

Her mood changed as soon as she crossed the avenue. A garbage truck had stopped a half block ahead of her. Her pickup was in the next can on its route. She dropped her bags and began running toward the truck.

Schaeffer was a block away when he saw her start running. He shouted to Jacobson. They ran a red light and swerved into a diagonal across Ninetieth Street. Schaeffer jumped out and tried to catch up with her.

She was about thirty yards ahead, hobbling badly. He yelled her name over and over as he ran but she didn't hear. The truck had just swallowed Margaret's pickup and the hydraulic compactor was beginning to move.

Schaeffer was catching up to Margaret, and when she finally heard him she stopped suddenly, about forty yards away from the truck. As she turned to look at him, an explosion ripped the steel shell of the truck in half, sending several tons of garbage rocketing out in all directions. The explosion blew Margaret off her feet and she collapsed into a heap on the pavement. Glass and wet mucuslike paper landed on top of her. Every window on the corner below the fourth story had been shattered, either from the shock wave, or from being pierced by the shooting garbage, and no flat surface within forty yards of the truck had been spared the spray. Nothing solid had hit Margaret and by the time Schaeffer came up, she was standing again, shaking. She had cut her hands in the fall and some blood trickled down her fingers.

Schaeffer looked her over quickly and told her to wait in the police car. Jacobson could fix her hands. Schaeffer picked his way farther down the block. A fire burned inside the two halves of the truck and a trail of black acrid smoke wafted through the opening and across the avenue.

One garbage man was sprawled motionless on the sidewalk. Schaeffer went over to him, felt for a pulse, and walked back to the truck.

Another man was hanging out of the cab on the driver's side and a thin line of blood seeped from his ear. There was nothing Schaeffer could do.

The usual cacophony of the area had stilled. People looked out their windows and hovered in doorways, but no one spoke. Schaeffer looked up and down both sides of the block but no one else had been hurt. He started to walk back to the car when he heard a low groan. He rushed toward it. A third truckman was lying under the front bumper. The thickness of the high cab and heavy front engine had saved him. His breathing was heavy and his eyes were glazed, but he was still alive. Schaeffer bent down to comfort him.

The thin wail of a siren filtered through the heavy silence and into Schaeffer's consciousness. Before long two police cars and an ambulance pulled up to the corner.

Schaeffer wanted to get away. In a few minutes the place would be mobbed and he didn't want to be the one to answer questions. Morley could handle it, he thought. He started picking his way back to the car past the police who were looking after the bodies and trying to keep back the growing crowd of spectators.

Schaeffer climbed into the front seat next to Margaret and told Jacobson to get the hell away. He lit a cigarette and looked over at Margaret. Her face was pale, her eyes studying him.

"That was meant for you," he said softly, taking her hands in his and making sure Jacobson had done a good job.

She leaned back and stared out of the front window. "In that case," she said, "I think you'd better tell me the whole story."

# Thirteen

MORLEY LEANED OVER THE DESK AND crushed out his cigarette.

"Well, that's about it," he said, straightening up and looking across at Margaret. He had tried to be as open with her as he could. "Now you know as much as we do. You can see we're at a dead end." He threw his hands up and glanced over at Schaeffer.

"Well, what's going to happen, then?" Margaret's face had regained its color but she was feeling irritated. Here was the great New York Police Department telling her that they'd been had. All the planning and all that work, and they were still at square one.

Morley shifted in his seat. "Well, it's obvious they'll change their tactics." He stood up and walked to the window. "It's my guess they'll lay low for a few weeks to wait for things to simmer down. By then, they'll have everything rearranged and start the stuff coming in again. They know now about our connection and I'm sure that their only fear is that you'll be able to spot one of them. They'll come after you again."

He turned from the window to look at her. "You'll have to move to a place where they can't find you. Today!"

"What," Margaret said. "Not go home?"

Schaeffer leaned over and placed his hand on her arm.

"Margaret, Lieutenant Morley's right. We have to get you out of that apartment, out of Manhattan even. You're dangerous to them."

"But that's my neighborhood, my friends."

"Forget about all that," Morley said. "The next time they won't be so careless and you won't need friends, except maybe to pay their last respects. Do you have any relatives or friends who live out of town?"

Margaret was silent for a moment. She knew they were right. But she could never move away. An idea was beginning to form in her mind and as she turned it over a smile slowly spread across her face.

"Yes, in fact, I do," she began. "Well, I have a nephew, John Foster, my sister's boy." She seemed to search her memory for a moment. "Last time we spoke he was living in Jackson Heights, 42 Ditman Avenue. He's always wanted me to visit with him, maybe I could stay a while until . . ."

"Call him," Morley said. "Tell him it's important." He pushed the phone across the desk.

She picked it up and dialed Queens Information. Margaret gave the name and waited. In a few seconds the operator came back and said she had no listing for that location. Margaret thanked her and hung up.

She looked up at Morley and beamed. "Still there . . . TW 4-7081. Should I call him now?"

"Yes."

She pulled the phone closer and dialed her own number. She let it ring once and started speaking.

"John, it's Margaret . . . Yes, John, I'm fine . . . You, too? . . . Good . . . good." She hesitated. "Well, that's nice. I'm glad to hear it. Listen, John, I wonder if I can spend some time at your place, it's important . . . will that be all right? . . . You will? Milly won't mind, you're sure? Oh, it's nothing. I'll explain when I see you. Later today . . . that's fine. Thanks, John."

She quietly placed the receiver back on its cradle and sighed deeply. "It's okay," she said, leaning back. "He said he'd be delighted."

"Well, that's settled," Morley said. "I'll send Jacobson over with you to help collect some of the things you need. Then you can take a cab to Queens. We will arrange to get the rest of your stuff to you after you've settled in. We'll get in touch with you at your nephew's." He looked down at the pad where he had scribbled down the number and address. "Fortunate he was still around," Morley said.

"Yes, wasn't it?" Margaret stood up. "I'll keep in touch too . . . and don't worry about me. I can take care of myself." She turned and winked at Schaeffer. "I'll just stay away from Uncle Charlies."

She said good-bye to Morley and left.

"Who the hell is Uncle Charlie?" Morley grumbled.

"The killer from *Shadow of a Doubt*. Specialized in lonely widows."

Morley shrugged.

"It's a private joke."

An hour later she had packed two suitcases and joined Jacobson in the lobby. He had a taxi waiting and Margaret squeezed herself in next to her two suitcases. Jacobson leaned through the window and wished her good luck. She gave the driver the Queens address and waved good-bye. Two blocks later, Margaret leaned forward and tapped the plexiglass behind the driver.

"Forget about that address in Queens," she ordered. "Take me to Broadway and Ninety-third Street."

# Fourteen

BERTIE WAS ABOUT TO GO OUT FOR her afternoon walk when she heard the knock and found Margaret standing awkwardly between two suitcases.

"Why, Margaret . . ."

"Bertie," Margaret began, "I must see you . . . so much has happened."

"Come in, come in," Bertie said. "You're not going away?" she asked.

"No, I can't." Her voice sounded a little strained. "They want me to, but I can't."

"Here, you just sit down and tell Bertie what's happened," she insisted. For the first time Bertie noticed the bandages on Margaret's hands.

"Oh, it's a long story," Margaret said. "It's awfully complicated. But, Bertie, I do need your help. You were so nice to me last night that I had this crazy idea."

Margaret leaned back into the soft couch. "I guess I should start when Rose told me about the money. It's hard to understand unless you get the whole picture."

For the next half hour Margaret narrated the story of the drug ring and her role in trying to uncover it. She talked about Schaeffer and Morley, about Sarah and Rose and the man from the laboratory whom they had found shot to death. Morley had been very thorough in his briefing and she was able to tell Bertie about their fake drop, the rifled lab files, and even the names of the garbage men who had been in league with Longley. At the end she described the explosion and for emphasis held up her hands to show Bertie.

Bertie did not take her eyes off Margaret during the entire story. She dared not even try to sort it out for fear she'd miss an important detail. She could hardly believe that something like this had happened to someone she knew, her friend, who was sitting next to her, right in her own apartment.

"And that's why they wanted me to leave," Margaret concluded. "But I couldn't, so I came here instead." She rose from the sofa. "Do you mind if I get myself some water?"

Bertie jumped up at the suggestion. "No, no, sit down, let me. You just rest. My Lord..." She rushed into the kitchen and came back in a few moments. "But, Margaret, I think they're right. It sounds very dangerous. But if you want you can stay here."

"Thanks, Bertie. I only hope it won't be long."

"Stay for as long as you like."

Margaret closed her eyes, wanting to forget about everything for a moment.

Bertie could hardly sit still. "Well, certainly you can't go out on the streets. I mean they're sure to have someone looking for you."

Margaret kept her eyes closed. "Yes, they probably will, and it'll probably be dangerous as long as those crooks are out there."

Bertie was confused. "I thought the police had run into a dead end..."

"Yes... they have." Margaret opened her eyes and turned to her friend. "But *I* haven't."

"You haven't?"

"No, and I think I know how to find them, but I'm going to need your help." She took a sip of water and placed the glass back on the table.

"Of course." Bertie's voice wavered just the slightest.

"But if you do find them . . . well . . . what could you do . . . what would you do with them?"

"Give the information to Sergeant Schaeffer. I'm sure he wouldn't let them slip away again. You see, his problem is finding them. If I'm right, we can find their headquarters, their names, and their contacts. With that kind of information, Sergeant Schaeffer would be able to make the arrests." She paused. "And then I could go back to my apartment. It's all very simple."

Bertie looked at her skeptically. "How are you going to find them?"

"Oh, they are bound to make a little mistake—at least, that's what I'm counting on." She smiled and looked around her. "But we have to get started right away . . . Do you have any other chairs? Enough for another eight people or so?"

Bertie was still puzzled. "Well, I guess we need three or four more. I can get them from Mrs. Jacobs next door."

"Good. While you get them, I'll make a list of people I want you to speak to. If possible, I want them all here by six this evening."

Bertie's eyebrows raised just a little.

"You don't mind do you?"

"No, I just wish I knew what you were planning."

"You'll find out tonight. It's already three o'clock and you'll have to hurry if you want to see all of them in time. You remember Rose, don't you?"

Bertie looked startled. "You mean that crazy old shopping-bag lady you introduced me to on the bench a few weeks ago?"

"Why, Bertie, I'm surprised you react that way to her. She's really very nice. You should have seen what I looked like last week. Rose will want to help. When you see her, tell her to come right away. You might find her at the center if she's not on the street."

Bertie got the extra chairs and set them up in the living room. She knew all the names on Margaret's list, and after she had made sure her friend was comfortable, she left to find Margaret's friends.

Margaret sprawled on the couch and closed her eyes.

She was wakened by the sound of someone fumbling with the door, and she got up to let Bertie in. Rose was standing next to her, looking very uneasy.

"She didn't want to come alone," Bertie said, her voice sounding tired. Bertie slowly walked into the apartment, kicked off her shoes, and let out a sigh of relief.

"I must have walked two miles," she began, "but I got everyone. They'll be here by six." She rubbed her feet together and bent over to massage her calves. "Roosa said he couldn't make it till seven, but I convinced him to get here on time. The old sot probably wanted a couple of drinks at Riley's before he came."

Margaret helped Rose to a chair.

"Eh, what's this all about then?" Rose asked.

"I have a little confession to make," Margaret began. "And I thought I'd tell you first—before the others. It sort of all begins with you . . ."

Ten minutes later, the explanation over, Margaret began to draw up the assignments. She left Rose on the chair, fidgeting with her bags and looking confused. It would be another hour before the others came, and it would be better to be prepared than have them quibble among themselves. She was a little nervous at the thought of all of them together at one time and in an unfamiliar setting, but they were her only resources.

Sid appeared at the door at five minutes to six.

"Look who I picked up in the lobby," he said, turning around to point to Durso, Alfonso, and Sophie. "They were waiting till the stroke of six." He laughed. "No need to be so formal, eh?" Looking around him, he noticed all the chairs and he turned to Bertie. "You didn't tell me this was going to be a party. Maybe we should arrange them all in a row so we feel more comfortable."

The doorbell rang again and Margaret let Roosa in. He was standing in the hallway, looking around guardedly. Two were still missing, Pancher Reese and Rena Bernstein. She'd wait. Five minutes later Rena arrived and cautiously walked into the room. She sat down quietly.

"Good to see you," Sid said, after introducing her around. "I see you brought your transistor."

Margaret directed a fierce glance at Sid. It was true that Rena listened to every talk show she could, but Margaret thought Sid's remark unnecessary. She wanted everyone to feel as comfortable as possible. The room quickly returned to the murmur of low conversations. None of them had any idea why they were there and questions flew around the room. Most of them were already seated, but Rose stood near the door. Of all the guests, she looked the most nervous, gathering her shopping bags around her as if they were her last wall of defense. Finally Pancher arrived and Margaret moved into the center of the room.

She looked around at her assembled friends. A ragged lot, she mused. There wasn't a new article of clothing among the group. Pancher wore a shirt that was past being frayed and his slacks were held up by a pair of suspenders attached to only three buttons. Rena's dress looked the nicest but it had been patched in several places. The smell of cheap musty perfume filled the room.

"I am not paranoid," Margaret began, "but I'd like to know if any of you thought you were followed here tonight." The room was silent, while they all looked at each other. Everyone shook their heads but no one spoke. "That's good," she continued, "we can't be too careful. Someone is trying to kill me and I'd rather not make it too easy for them."

Sid shifted in his chair and rubbed his two-day beard. "Could you repeat that?"

"Yes. Someone is trying to kill me and I need your help or else they'll probably get me." Everyone started talking at once. She had opened on as strong a note as possible, hoping it would set the tone and keep everyone interested. Now she'd have to convince them.

"Let me explain. Over six weeks ago I agreed to help the police with an investigation." She looked over as Rose clutched tighter on one of her bags. "I don't know why I did it. I guess I was just crazy. Anyway, we thought, or rather they thought, it would be finished within a month, maybe six weeks at most. I went along also because the people they were investigating are the worst, the lowest criminals." She paused to let it sink in. "Not only are they importing drugs into this city, but they're also a bunch of murderers. They killed Sarah Feiner because they thought she had crossed them. Maybe some of you knew her." There were murmurs in the room.

"She wasn't killed by a robber as the papers reported. The police wanted the murderers to think they had been fooled. The false report enabled me to take over where Sarah had stopped."

"Where was that?" Roosa interrupted.

"As a runner of drug payments. I've been doing that for the last six weeks in the hopes we could uncover their operation. I won't get involved in details, but yesterday our plan backfired when the man the police thought would lead them to the organization was found murdered." She looked around at her friends. "Well, apparently I was next on their list."

"Whadda ya mean?" Roosa asked.

"Here, give me that," Margaret said. She motioned to the folded evening paper Pancher was holding on his lap. She flipped it open and held it up. The headline read "Garbage Truck Explodes. Two killed." Underneath was a picture of the jagged truck. "Let's just say I was lucky."

The nine other people in the room looked at the picture, then at Margaret.

"If it was me they were after I'd be in Kansas by now," Durso said. "What're you hanging around for?"

"Because I don't like being told where to live. Besides, if the police are stymied, I'm not. I think I know how to find them. All I need is your help." She sat down and folded her hands. "It will mean a few days of your time. I have to find something and you're the only ones I know who can help."

The room was silent until Sid spoke up. "Margaret, it's a hell of a story. I'd hate to miss the ending. What do you want us to find?"

"I want you to look inside garbage cans, hundreds of them. I'm looking for something that only these criminals have. When we find it, we've found them. It means hours of searching through the cans belonging to every brownstone and every apartment house over a large area. They may have gotten rid of it already. Then, again, they may not even be in this part of town, although I have a feeling they are. This morning one of them mentioned to me he knew this area . . . knew how long it would take to get from one place to another. It's my only hope. If it doesn't work, then I'll have to move away and probably never see you all again. Now." She looked around her. "I can understand how some of you may be reluctant to get involved. God knows it's not a pleasant job. But it would make it so much easier if some of you could help." There was silence for a moment.

Roosa was the first to move. He stood up, looking a little embarrassed. "Margaret, I've known you for a good many years. Most of the time you seemed a little blurred to me, but that was my own fault." He smiled. "If you want to use my eyes, however unfocused they may be at times, they're yours." He sat down.

"Thank you," Margaret said. "Sid, you too?"

"Sure."

"And me." Rose left her bags and moved farther toward the group. "Got the most experience."

It didn't take long for the other six to join in. It was the first time they'd been asked for help, the first time they'd been needed.

"Oh, thank you." Margaret smiled. "I knew my friends would be with me when I needed them." She went to the table and picked up her list of assignments. "I prepared a little chart. Now, there's nine of you. I thought of starting on Eightieth Street and going to Ninety-sixth. We'll cover it from the Park to Riverside Drive. That's eighty square blocks, or roughly nine blocks apiece. It's a lot of work and will probably take you all day." She read out their names and told them which blocks to cover. "Try not to be too conspicuous, and report back here every evening at around six. But if any of you find what we're looking for, I want you to call me right away and then go back and keep an eye on the can until I arrive. I think I can risk one quick trip. Needless to say, if anyone asks about me while you're out, you don't know anything. Even to the police." She looked at her watch. "Any questions?"

"Just one," Sid said. "Exactly what are we looking for?"

Margaret's face turned red. "Imagine," she grinned, "forgetting the most important detail."

Margaret spent the next day alone in Bertie's apartment. She finished off the morning's crossword, paced the floor, and waited for the phone to ring. Several times she was tempted to go out and look on her own, but she never made it farther than the front door. Once the right can was spotted she'd have to carry out her plan and she didn't want to miss the call.

Bertie came home at 12:30. The only person she had seen on the street was Rena—with*out* her transistor radio. Rena had never been parted from her transistor as long as they had known her. "She hasn't found anything. Me neither," Bertie said as she sat down heavily. "I've done five of them." She looked up at Margaret. "Four more to go. No time for the pigeons today . . . I guess they'll have to take care of themselves."

Margaret promised that if they found what they were looking for she would buy three large cans of spicy Italian bread crumbs and give a party for Bertie's pigeons. Bertie seemed pleased at the suggestion.

Bertie left again after lunch and Margaret sat down near the phone. The chances of finding it weren't very good. The more time that went by, the lower the odds. She decided to limit the search to three days. If they hadn't found it by then, she'd call it off. Then they could all go back to

their benches. Only there would be one difference, one less
face . . . hers. She looked down at the phone, willing it to
ring. Her patience was wearing thin and it was still only
the first day. She picked up the day's crossword again to
make sure that all her entries were correct.

Ten minutes later the phone rang. Margaret was so anxious she pounced on it almost before the first ring had
ended.

It was Sid. "Just thought you'd like to know I decided
not to take the bus. Show you how hard I'm working."

"Bus! Sid, what bus?"

"The bus to Belmont," he replied, "to see the Greeley
Stakes. Go every year but I decided I'd miss it . . . still
have three blocks to do. Just didn't want you to think I'm
goofing off."

Good old Sid, she thought, has just taken a year off my
life. "Did you find anything yet?" The question was hope-
ful but she knew that if he had anything he would have told
her.

"Nope. Still looking."

"Okay, Sid, I appreciate it . . . your missing the race, but
next time save your call for the real thing!"

Sid caught the tone in her voice and apologized.
"Sorry," he said. "Thought you'd like to know. See you
later."

She hung up and rested her head on the back of the
chair. Something was happening to all her friends. Rena
had left her radio home. Bertie wasn't interested in her
pigeons, and Sid had missed a favorite race. It was the
kind of enthusiasm she had hoped for, but never really
expected. It made her realize there was still a possibility.
All this energy. If only it paid off.

Around six o'clock her friends started dropping by. One
by one they trudged and shuffled into Bertie's apartment,
their bodies exhausted and their clothes stained. Pancher
looked the worst. He collapsed on the couch and closed his
eyes for two minutes before speaking.

"Maybe we find it tomorrow," he offered.

Margaret looked at him with gratitude. He was almost

seventy-five, and certainly unused to such a tiring day. Yet he refused to give up. Such a good friend and she'd probably never be able to see him again if the search didn't work.

"Pancher, if it's too much, you don't . . ."

"No, no. It's just my eyes." He got up to leave. "They get a little tired, that's all. Water a lot, you know." He patted her arm. "We find him tomorrow, hey, don't worry." She pressed his hand and let him out.

Rose was the last to show up.

"Nine blocks of cans," Margaret asked, "and not a single thought for yourself?" She was surprised that Rose had come without her bags and almost didn't recognize her.

"'leven," Rose corrected her. "Had a little time left so's I went below Eightieth. Didn't find nothin' though. Anyone else?"

Margaret shook her head, still impressed with Rose's performance. "No, not yet," she sighed. "Maybe tomorrow."

"Well, if it's there, we'll find it." She winked at her friend. "You'll see, we'll get it."

Margaret couldn't help feeling a little better. Rose's enthusiasm was catching. "I hope so," she replied. "You've all been so wonderful. I'd hate . . ."

"Aw, come on!" Rose exclaimed. "No diff'rent than a reg'lar day for me. See ya tomorrow at six."

# Fifteen

"NO, THERE IS NO JOHN FOSTER LISTED at 42 Ditman Avenue. And all of the Fosters in Jackson Heights never heard of Margaret Binton."

Morley exploded. "What!"

"Not one."

"What about the phone number she got from Information?"

"A florist shop." Schaeffer got up and leaned against the wall. "No dice. That whole thing was for our benefit. I thought she gave in too easily."

Morley lowered his eyes to the phone. "Christ, what the hell for? She'll get herself killed."

Schaeffer shrugged. "I don't think she liked the idea of being forced out. Can't really blame her."

"So where the hell is she?" Morley got up and walked to the window.

"My guess is she's staying with some friend, waiting till things blow over."

"They're not going to blow over." Morley turned to Schaeffer. "The way this fucking investigation is going she'll wind up in the river."

"Yeah, so I gotta find her, and it won't be easy. She could be any number of places. I don't know her friends. I suppose I could check out the benches—see if anyone knows her."

"Just a minute. What about Rose Gaffery?"

"Oh, yeah. She was the one that found the money," Schaeffer said.

"Also try to find the cabbie who picked Margaret up in front of her apartment. Ask Jacobson about the time."

"What about putting a stakeout on her apartment?"

"Why don't you just check it daily? I don't think she'd be that foolish—it's too soon, and we just don't have the manpower."

Schaeffer frowned.

"Listen, don't get me wrong," Morley said. "I like Margaret but we got to keep the pressure up on breaking this operation. Any leak, any hint . . ." Morley paused to light a cigarette. "Staunton's checking on the landlord who rented the building to Longley. I know it's thin, but the guy is supposed to have some gambling contacts." He lifted his arms toward the ceiling. "Who knows? What else can I do?"

Schaeffer started fidgeting. "I better get going."

"Yeah, and if you find her, bring her right in. Don't let her sweet-talk you like before."

# Sixteen

EARLY THE NEXT MORNING MARGARET
made a quick trip to the corner store to buy another book of
thirty crossword puzzles. She was intrigued by its promise
to "baffle and tease." She walked back to Bertie's in the
early morning sun, making sure that no one was following
her. She guessed Morley and Schaeffer would also be
looking for her. Poor Schaeffer, Margaret thought. I hope
he won't be too mad. There was still some hot coffee in the
pot and Margaret settled back with a cup and her new
book. The puzzles were easier than the ones in the daily
paper, and she quickly finished the first two. She turned to
the back of the book in the hope that they got harder, but in
fact the last puzzle was easier than the first. When it was
close to noon Margaret got up to prepare some lunch.

The whole thing was foolish, she thought as she struggled with the can opener. There were too many areas of
uncertainty and she was counting on the mob's careless-
ness, the one thing they had never shown. They had made
the police look like amateurs. She was beginning to feel
guilty for creating so much hard work for her friends.
Maybe it was even useless work. And all she was doing
was sitting back filling in puzzles.

Bertie came in looking tired and was unusually quiet at
the table, commenting only on the weather. Margaret, too,

was silent. It's not fair, she kept thinking, not fair. And there were eight others, each one as tired and undone as the next. She looked up at Bertie.

"Today's the last day. If you see any of the others, let them know."

Bertie looked puzzled. "But we haven't found it yet. We shouldn't stop till we do."

"It's no use, it's not there. I had hopes it might be, but . . ."

"What's this?" Bertie shook her head. "I know it's hard on you, but it's no good unless we continue, at least for another day. You'll see." She sipped her coffee. "And if you're thinking about us, forget it. It's tiring, but in the end, at night, it's a wonderful feeling. Plus, we're all doing something together. It's sort of exciting really." She was quiet for several minutes when she finished the coffee.

"But Bertie . . ."

"You just have to leave it to us," Bertie said. She waited until Margaret nodded, then opened the door and went out to finish her last four blocks. Margaret shrugged and went back to her crosswords.

The scene at six was the same as the previous evening. Everyone dragged themselves in, reported no luck and offered consolation. Margaret told each one that the next day would be the last. Sid suggested that they continued until the end of the week, but Margaret wouldn't hear of it. All her friends looked more worn down than they had the previous evening and she knew that one more day was all she could ask for. That evening she and Bertie watched TV for a few hours and went to bed early.

Margaret woke up at eight o'clock and looked out the window. A heavy rain was falling. Bertie had already left, and Margaret suspected she had snuck out to avoid being disuaded. It was too late to contact everyone and call it off. She felt so guilty.

After breakfast she sat down again with her crossword book. The steady sounds of the rain on the window and of the wind sweeping around the building destroyed all her concentration and her eyes blurred the words. By ten o'clock she was dozing, her hand still clutching the pencil and resting lightly on the open book in her lap.

The ringing of the phone woke her up. Still holding the pencil, she turned and lifted the receiver.

"I think I've found it. Margaret . . . are you there?"

"Who is this?" she asked, not sure she had heard correctly.

"It's Pancher, Margaret. I think I've found it, just like you said."

"Where are you? Where's the can?"

"It's on Ninety-third just off Central Park West. About fifty yards from the avenue, south side. Group of about twelve cans from a large apartment building."

"Okay. Quick, go back and wait. I'll be right there. Stay out of sight. If anyone comes to empty that can, delay them."

"Okay," Pancher said, "but hurry." In less than five minutes Margaret was heading uptown in a taxi.

The cans were in the service alley. Pancher appeared from behind a corner and walked quickly to her side.

"It's this one," he said, lifting off the top of the nearest can. He pointed inside. "There, take a look."

She gently brushed aside some paper and an empty box of Ritz crackers and exposed the yellow plastic package. Pancher had already opened it and she could just make out the white substance inside. She put a finger through the opening and pulled it back to her tongue. "That's it," she said, tasting sugar. Pancher's face was beaming. "Did you move things around a lot?"

"Not at all," he said. "You can see it's near the top."

"That's good. Now," she turned around, "we have to get it all to Bertie's."

Pancher looked puzzled. "The whole thing?"

"Yes. Here, give me a hand." She replaced the lid, pushing it down firmly, and grabbed one of the handles on the side of the can. "Wait, better check if anybody's coming." Pancher looked cautiously out of the alley and pulled his head back in.

"No, no one nearby."

"Good, here." She picked up one side of the metal can and Pancher lifted the other. They managed to walk about one hundred feet before they had to put it down. She thought of hailing a taxi but didn't think any cabbie would stop for them. She made sure that they set down the can near the garbage bins of a brownstone to avoid looking too suspicious. They waited until the way was clear before they continued. If someone passed them while they were carrying it, they just lowered their heads and kept going. New Yorkers were used to strange sights, and Margaret hoped that she and Pancher would just fit in with the rest of the oddities.

"How are you doing?" she asked as they approached Broadway.

"Let's rest a bit," he said. "This next haul will be bad."

They were still fifty feet from the curb and had to make it across Broadway in one dash. She wanted to stop at least thirty feet down the next street. From there it was only one more short empty block. They slid the can next to another one and huddled in the brownstone's front vestibule. Pancher was drenched. He wiped his face with a handkerchief and gave Margaret a broad smile.

"We get him back," he said. "No worries."

She patted his shoulder and leaned against the wall. She was breathing heavily and could feel her heart pounding against her rib cage. Most exercise I've had in my whole life, she thought.

She stepped outside to glance across Broadway. For the first time she noticed the police car double-parked next to a coffee shop at the corner. A policeman was in the driver's seat smoking a cigarette. The last thing she wanted now was to see Morley. He'd probably put her under armed escort and send her to Buffalo, or Rochester. She walked back into the vestibule and shook her head.

Pancher was shaking with cold. She was worried about him and decided that they would have to go, police or no police. They grabbed the can and started walking at a snail's pace. The police car was no longer there and Margaret looked around nervously until she saw it stopped for a red light a block away. Margaret found it hard to walk straight and stumbled over her own feet once or twice. Pancher's whole body was straining with the effort. Two or three people glanced at them, but either the rain or an inbred urban indifference kept them on their way. Another twenty feet and they would be safe.

"Over here," she said, but at that moment she felt Pancher's grip loosen and the can hit the sidewalk. It took all her strength to keep it upright.

"Sorry," he said, "I couldn't hold it no longer." He rubbed his hands together to get the circulation going again. She looked around her. The can was sitting about ten feet in from the curb in the middle of the corner. People crossing the street had to detour around it. It was an embarrassing moment. Any second she was sure someone would come over and make a scene, but no one did.

They made it to Bertie's building with only one more stop, and after they had dragged the can into the apartment, Pancher collapsed on the couch. Margaret insisted he take a hot bath and she drew the water and all but pushed him into the bathroom.

"And afterward," Margaret said, "I want you to get into Bertie's bed while your clothes are drying." He smiled at her and agreed, too tired to argue. Margaret put on the kettle, changed her clothes, and nestled into the couch with a cup of hot tea. The trophy of their hunt stood in front of her in the middle of the living room, as if on display .353 C.P.W. was printed on its side in thick black lettering.

Well, she smiled to herself. I think their little game is up!

# Seventeen

MARGARET WAS STILL EXCITED WHEN Bertie arrived for lunch, and before Bertie had even sat down she started relating the story of their trek. As soon as they had eaten, Margaret asked Bertie to find their friends and tell them to stop searching.

"Ask them to come by around six," she added. "I wouldn't want them to miss the best part."

Margaret had the afternoon to spend alone with the garbage can. She could hear Pancher's snoring in the next room but didn't want to wake him. She made a quick tour of the living room and cleared out the one small throw rug, some small chairs, and a footstool, leaving the dining-room table, the couch, and an end table, which she moved to the side wall. She slowly began removing the contents of the can and laid them out on the floor in neat rows, working from left to right, smoothing out and placing every scrap of garbage in its proper place. When she had finished her sorting she had four rows with a walkway a foot wide between each row. From the grid she had fashioned she could tell where each item of garbage had been in the can: what articles were above it, near it, or below it. The sugar was at the end of the first row, with the Ritz cracker box slightly to its left.

An hour later she had finished the first step of her plan

and leaned back on the couch to survey her work. Crumpled scraps of paper, discarded envelopes, wrinkled soggy magazines and newspapers, several empty aluminum soda cans, cigarette butts, used tissues, food scraps—Margaret sighed at the prospect that lay ahead of her: the hard part, figuring out what belonged to whom.

Though she was exhausted, she dragged herself up from the couch and over to the top of the left-hand row. She dropped to her knees and approached the task like an archaeologist, making associations and taking notes.

She found five different names on the envelopes and magazines. One of the names belonged to a minister and she ruled him out. She couldn't bring herself to admit the possibility that a man of the Church was involved in a drug run, a man who subscribed to *Guidepost* magazine and read it through carefully, making notes on several pages.

Unfortunately, the envelopes near the sugar were addressed to more than one individual. Of the remaining four names, three were equally represented in the first and second rows. The fourth person, a Mr. Tompkins, had one envelope in the third row and two in the last. She didn't rule him out but she thought him a doubtful suspect. She couldn't eliminate any of the remaining three names. None of the return addresses were significant and she could find no other clues. She wrote out her final list of names, putting an X next to the minister's, a question mark next to Tompkins, and brackets around the last three: Sam Moorman, Richard Jauner, and Max Daker.

By 6:30 everyone had arrived and were talking excitedly to each other. Pancher, who had come out of Bertie's room dressed and clean, held the center of attention. He described in detail to each new arrival how he had discovered the parcel. They all agreed he had been a hero. Margaret and Bertie had cleaned up the trash before the meeting, but the can was proudly displayed in the entrance hall. Durso and Roosa were asked to return it the next day, but to cover it with a large plastic bag to avoid any confrontations.

Margaret thanked her friends. "It wasn't only Pancher,"

she said. "Without all of you, we never would have found it, but there's still a little more work to do. The final touches. It won't be difficult and I guarantee you'll enjoy the ending."

Margaret explained how far she had gotten. She now needed to find out which of the three or four men had thrown out the sugar.

"Why don't you just give the police the names you have?" Durso interrupted. "Let them work it out."

"Why should I run the risk they'll muck up everything like the last time? Besides," she smiled, "I need to present them with the final answer or else they'll get angry at me for disappearing. It won't be too hard."

Durso looked skeptical.

"I need something simple and exact . . . and quick," she continued.

"You want us to snoop around their doorways?" Rena asked. "I could always say I was somebody's cook. They'd never suspect."

"No, something even better." Margaret turned to Sid. "Didn't you once tell me you had a friend who works in a printing shop?"

Sid nodded. "Still does."

"Good. Do you think he'd print some flyers for you? We need only four."

"Sure, I'm always doing him favors, putting his bets on."

"Well, then, if some of you could just spend another day. Not all of you." She looked around. "I think six would do . . . to be on the safe side."

Roosa cleared his throat. "What did you have in mind, Margaret?"

"Here, let me ask you a question," she replied. Her gaze swept the whole room. "What would you all do if you received an invitation to take . . . let's say . . . scuba diving lessons at a five-dollar discount? Something you weren't interested in and couldn't use?"

"I'd probably throw it out," Roosa said. "I can't even swim."

"Precisely. But what if you had just hidden something underwater using a scuba outfit? Wouldn't you be curious about the coincidence of getting the announcement in the mail?"

Roosa thought for a moment. "Yes."

"And don't you think you'd check on the announcement to see if it was a legitimate coincidence or something more threatening?"

"Yes, probably, but I don't see what this all has to do with drugs."

"I do," Sid said. He looked over at Margaret for confirmation. "We send each of the people on your list an announcement which is meaningless to everyone but the guy you want. Everyone throws them out but him, right?"

"Right." Margaret's eyes were shining. "All we have to do is follow them to see which one goes to check on the announcement. Then we'll know for sure."

"You're a smart'un," Rose said.

"Thank you." Margaret blushed slightly. "Now we have to figure out what to send. It can't be too obvious. Let's see." She thought for a moment. "What if we send them all an announcement of a special at the A & P, a special on Domino Sugar and plastic garbage bags?"

"Subtle," Sid laughed. "Very subtle."

"But do you think they'd notice it?" Durso asked.

"I think so," Margaret said. "We'll go to Sid's friend tomorrow morning and get him to print the flyers, but we'll have to wait until Monday to deliver them. Pancher, you can do that, their apartment numbers are on my list. Just walk in and tell the elevator man you have flyers to deliver for the Cancer Fund. I'm sure he'll let you go up; they do it in my building all the time. The rest of you can wait outside for them to come out. Whoever goes to the A & P right away is our man. Any questions?"

"Just one," Roosa said. "How are we going to know who they are? We've never seen any of them before and it's a large building. Pancher can't stay up there very long. How could he signal us?"

"Oh." Margaret frowned. "I hadn't thought of that."

"Well, it's important," Roosa continued. "We can't follow everyone who comes out of the building!"

"Wait a minute." Sid stood up. "Isn't there a doorman in that building?"

"I think there is," Pancher said. "Yes, a doorman in a brown uniform."

"Well then, it's easy," Sid continued. "We'll just make it worth his while to tip us off."

"Bribery?" Margaret grinned. "Sid, sometimes I wonder about you." She thought for a moment. "Would it work?"

"I think so," he said. "Those guys don't make that much and it's really no trouble for him. All he has to do is tip his hat or something like that." He paused." Of course, we'd have to make it a sufficient amount . . ."

"How much?" Margaret questioned.

"It's how much we can spare," Sid went on. He opened his own frayed wallet and pulled out one five and eight singles. "I need about ten to hold me until the end of the month, so here's three from me." He looked around at the others.

Rena fumbled in her handbag until she found her wallet. She thought for a moment and finally withdrew $1.82.

Rose took off a shoe and lifted the heel pad. She caught the edge of a five dollar bill and pulled it out.

"For a rainy day," she sighed, and tossed it on the table. The others were searching in their own special hiding places.

When it was all over they had $26.34, most of it in coins.

Sid shook his head. "A little shy. Let's hope it works. I'll change it all into singles so it looks bigger."

Margaret laughed. "Let's meet here on Monday morning to coordinate everything. I think my friends down at the police department will be pleased I didn't go to Queens."

# Eighteen

"I WISH SHE HAD GONE TO QUEENS," Morley sighed. "Even Brooklyn. Anywhere. I should have known better than to let her take that cab all by herself." He looked annoyed. "So where did he drop her off?"

Schaeffer glanced at his notes. "On the corner of Ninety-third and Broadway. He didn't hang around long enough to see which way she went."

"No address?"

"Nope." Schaeffer slid back in the chair. "Just Ninety-third and Broadway. He even forgets which corner."

"That doesn't help us too much. Did you find anyone who knows her? How about Rose Gaffery?"

"No one on the benches knew her, and I couldn't get hold of Gaffery."

"Hasn't been back to the center either?" Morley asked.

Schaeffer shook his head.

"Well, what can we do? How long do you think it would take you to check all the apartments within a block radius from Ninety-third Street?"

Schaeffer grimaced. "Maybe a week and even then we wouldn't be sure. We couldn't get into some of the apartments. She might see who it is and not open the door."

"All right," Morley interrupted. "You're better off finding Gaffery and checking the benches. I've had Jacobson

100

cruising for the past two days looking for Margaret. I'll tell him to stay around Ninety-third and Broadway. Maybe he'll spot her."

"Has he ever seen Gaffery?"

"I don't think so."

Schaeffer smiled. "But what the hell, she must be pretty obvious on the streets. Why don't you ask Jacobson to stop any scavengers and find out if they're Gaffery."

"You're right. As long as he's sitting there."

"What about the landlord, the one that rented the building to Longley?"

"Forget it. Nothing. The guy runs in a fast crowd, that's all. Bets a lot but mostly horses. He runs a legitimate real estate business. Owns three or four small factory buildings and one apartment house in the Bronx. He found out we were checking up on him and he was pissed. Staunton had a hard time with him at first."

"Why's he pissed? There was a murder in one of his buildings," Schaeffer pointed out.

"That's what Staunton told him and he finally opened up. Longley merely answered an ad he had placed in *The New York Times*. They knew no one in common, and he had never seen Longley or any of his associates before or after the lease was signed. Longley had been renting the place for about a year and was a prompt payer. That's all he knew." Morley threw up his hands. "Another fucking dead end. It's getting so I don't feel right about picking up my paycheck anymore."

"At least we have one consolation," Schaeffer said. "If we can't find her they can't either."

"Yeah, I've heard that one before too," Morley growled. "Last time just before the garbage truck exploded."

# Nineteen

SID CAME TO PICK UP MARGARET ON Saturday morning at ten. He could have gone to the printer's alone, but Margaret was insistent. She was anxious to get out of the apartment after being cooped up for four days.

Sid had put on a special outfit for the occasion: his best pair of pants and his most colorful shirt, a cotton print that bore a close resemblance to a racing flag. Margaret stifled a grin as she opened the door for him. The weather was still a little overcast, but it had turned warmer and they decided to carry umbrellas rather than coats. As they were about to leave Bertie took Sid aside and in a lowered voice insisted that he be extra careful on their trip. She pressed her remaining five dollars into his hand before he had time to complain.

"You take cabs . . . you understand," she cautioned. "Don't be cheap."

He look scandalized and quickly put the bill back down on her dining table. "But of course, Bertie . . . You didn't think I'd take a chance with Margaret. Don't worry, she'll be perfectly safe with me."

Margaret caught the last part of Sid's statement and grabbed his arm playfully. "Come on, save the crowing for later on." She winked at Bertie. "Cute, isn't he?"

They got a cab right away and drove downtown. It was a small shop in the low seventies off Amsterdam, the kind that specialized in short-run business, mostly one-sheet announcements and advertisements. The whole place was the size of a small candy store and might have been one previously—on top of one wall a peeling decal read "Drink Nehi."

Sid walked over to the man by the Xerox machine and waited until he had turned around.

"Where's Driscoll?" he asked casually.

"Be back in a minute," the man said.

Sid turned to talk to Margaret when he saw his friend walk in. They shook hands and Sid introduced Margaret. After a few pleasantries, Sid told him why they were there and gave him the copy.

"Some kind of joke?" Driscoll laughed.

"Just print it like I told you," Sid said, "if you want any more tips from me."

Driscoll smiled and nodded. "How large you want it?"

Margaret indicated with her hands. "This size. Can you do it?"

Driscoll took the paper and went behind his desk. "Sure. You only want four?" They both nodded. He looked at the clock on the wall. "Okay, come back in an hour." He pointed a finger at Sid. "And it's this fast only because you gave me that horse in the Greeley."

Margaret stole a glance at Sid as they left the shop.

"Don't worry," he remarked as they stepped out on the pavement. "I had it at O.T.B., too." He gestured down the street. "Let's get some coffee while we wait."

After an hour, a lot of conversation, and three cups of coffee, they returned to the printing shop. The place was empty except for the two employees. Driscoll was working over a press, his hands smudged with black ink.

"Another minute," he said as he made a small adjustment to the machine. He bent over and pulled a sheet off the top of the stack and handed it to Sid. "How's that?" Margaret peered over his shoulder and studied the paper.

"It's fine," she answered, "just what I had in mind."

She looked at Sid. "What do you think? Look authentic enough?"

Sid studied it a bit longer. He held it out as far as his arm could hold it, his eyes squinting. He rubbed his thumb over the ink. "Yeah, I guess so. How much do I owe you?" Sid asked, reaching tentatively into his pocket.

"Nothing, nothing." Driscoll shook his head. "Just make sure when you get some more inspiration you let me in on it. Anywhere, Aqueduct, Belmont . . . I'm flexible."

Sid winked at him. "If I hear anything you'll be the first to know." He steered Margaret to the door and quickly waved good-bye. "Must have made a killing," he said when they were outside. "He's usually not so agreeable."

They both laughed and started walking west. Sid had his eye open for another cab, but Margaret insisted on walking at least as far as Broadway. She complained of not getting enough fresh air. "Anyway, I'm not worried with you here."

He knew she was just flattering him but he enjoyed it. He smiled and told her she was taking unfair advantage, and led her toward Broadway.

Sid stepped out at the corner to flag down a taxi. With a series of stadium whistles and arm movements, it wasn't long before he had summoned a cab and opened its door, ready to usher Margaret in, but when he looked up, Margaret had disappeared. His eyes darted back up the block but it was empty. Broadway itself was crowded with people. Could she have been dragged away? His mind raced with all the dreadful possibilities.

"Hey, mac, you getting in?"

Sid looked back at the cab and slammed the door shut. "Sorry," he called as the cab sped away with a loud squeal. He looked around again, panicked, but saw a momentary opening in a group of pedestrians and spotted her entering a store about five doors away. "Thank God," he breathed and hurried after her.

The smell of smoked fish and fresh bagels wafted out onto the pavement even before he entered Rebach's Delicatessen and Food Emporium. He elbowed his way into the crowd and found Margaret in a line at the lox counter.

Mund had been sitting in a bar across the street when he saw Margaret enter the store. He was talking to the bartender but stopped in the middle of his sentence, laid five dollars on the counter, and rushed out.

There must have been about sixty people in the place when Mund entered. They were spread out at various counters, waiting in lines and milling about. Sausages and salamis were hanging from the ceiling and the noise level equaled the smell in intensity. People at the counters were yelling their orders. "No, no . . . too pale!" he heard some-one say as he moved farther into the store. A woman to his left was grumbling to a counterman about the size of the slices. "Too thick, too thick." He stopped next to the smoked cheeses and waited. Out of the corner of his eye he spotted Margaret. She was holding an umbrella and a small bag and pointing to a large slice of reddish fish.

"No, Marty, that one," she insisted. The man behind the counter shrugged his shoulders, replaced the piece he had already taken out, and pulled out the one she was pointing to. Mund moved closer and watched. Not here, he thought to himself. I'll get her outside.

Margaret watched Marty slice into the lox, a present for Bertie. She smiled apologetically at Sid, who was standing next to her in line and doing his best to look displeased, although he was relieved she hadn't been kidnapped.

She moved a step to the right to get a better view of Marty's handiwork and glanced at the mirror above the counter. Her hand tightened around the umbrella when she saw Mund's reflection.

He was watching her. She remembered the face from somewhere and felt anxious about the way he was staring at her, his eyes unwavering. It was not the look of someone waiting in Rebach's to buy smoked fish, she thought.

"Is that all?" Marty asked, placing the wrapped-up fish on the countertop.

"Uh . . . no." She flushed slightly. "Let me have some baked salmon . . . quarter pound." She was trying to figure out what she could do. She waited until Marty brought out a large piece and then told him she wanted it cut from the other fish. The other people in line were beginning to grumble but she paid no attention. She needed time to think.

"And a small whitefish . . . not too dried out."

Sid moved closer to whisper in her ear. "I thought you only wanted some lox?" he said.

"Don't look back," she said. "Someone's following . . . back there in the store." She felt Sid's hand grip her elbow.

"Where?"

"Next to the halvah."

Sid looked up into the mirror. The man was still there, still waiting.

"Anything else?" Marty said.

"No. That's all." She pulled out a ten-dollar bill and handed it over the counter. When she got the change she walked over to the meat department, only a few steps away. Sid was still holding her elbow.

"What should we do?" he whispered nervously. She could see he was beginning to perspire.

"Well, he can't shoot me here," she mumbled. "Not with all these people, not in Rebach's!"

"Can I help you?" the man behind the counter asked.

"Quarter pound of pastrami, please . . . make it lean." This can't go on, she thought to herself. I can't buy out the store, waiting. She moved closer to Sid and began whispering to him.

Sid moved away and disappeared into an aisle at the back of the store. The pastrami was handed over and Margaret stuffed it into the bag with the fish. She fumbled with her money for a minute, passed over three bills, pocketed the change, and slowly headed for the front door.

Mund started to follow her, but someone seized his wrist from behind and pulled him back.

"Stop him! He stole my wallet! Thief!" Sid dropped his wallet to the floor and continued screaming.

Margaret took a quick look over her shoulder and hurried out into the street.

Everyone in the store turned in the direction of the shouts.

"Help me! Don't let him get away," Sid yelled. "See, there's the wallet," he pointed.

"Let go, you crazy son-of-a-bitch," Mund screamed at Sid. Two men grabbed Mund's other arm and twisted it behind him while a small knot of people gathered around, making it impossible for him to muscle his way to the door.

The manager barged into the circle. "You both better come with me," he said. "We can talk about this in my office. Let him go," he said, jerking his head toward Mund.

The men released Mund to the manager but Mund was too quick and put his right hand into his belt and pulled out his revolver.

"I don't want to shoot anyone," Mund said. "So, don't anyone try to stop me." He held the gun at arm's length, pointing it at the nearest customer's head. He took a few steps, and then switched targets, slowly making his way to the door. His eyes searched the room for Sid, but Sid had ducked behind a counter. "I'll take care of you later, Grandpa," he called as he turned and rushed out into the street.

Margaret had been frantically searching for a taxi, but three long minutes passed before she finally found one. As she got in and turned around to make sure she was safe, she saw Mund searching the street.

He had seen her get into the cab and watched as it pulled down a side street. When an old, battered van with a psychedelic mural painted on its side slowed to a stop next to him, he rushed up to it and opened the door, pointing his gun at the bearded, shaggy young driver as he jumped in.

"Turn right," he said, pushing the muzzle into the driver's stomach.

"Hey, man . . ."

"Move it. And shut up," Mund said.

The driver shifted into first, went out through the red light, and swung right. He glanced nervously at the gun and then toward Mund. "Okay, man, you're the boss," he said. "Where to?"

"Make a right at the next block. Should be a cab ahead of you, maybe a block. One person in the back seat." Mund leaned out of the side window as they made the turn. "There it is." He sank back into the seat. "Follow them. And not too close," he added. "Don't try to be a hero."

The driver nodded and drove ahead. After a minute of silence he glanced sideways. "You a cop or something?"

"Shut up. Just keep driving."

Mund thought over his choices. He could overtake her and try to shoot through the window, or wait until she got out. "Close it up a little," he directed. "That's it, nice and easy."

Margaret sank down lower, pushing her knees against the back of the driver's seat. He was back there somewhere, following her. She was sure of it. Maybe in a cab, maybe in a car, but he was there. She looked down at the only possible weapons she had, a small red umbrella and a bag of smoked fish and pastrami. For the first time since she had gone into hiding she felt the awful reality of her position. Someone was trying to kill her. It had been a game until she had seen Mund inside Rebach's. God knows what happened to Sid, she thought. She imagined him lying wounded on the floor of the delicatessen, clutching the bagels and the grocery flyers. She should never have gotten everyone involved. She had tried to help the police, but now she had put all of her friends in danger. She had told the cabbie to just drive around, but now she wondered where she could go. Not to Bertie's. That was obvious. She could go to the police, but that meant she'd be sent away without being able to follow through. Everyone would still be unsafe.

She leaned forward and tapped on the partition. "Go right on Eighty-eighth to the Park. Then go downtown. I'll let you know where." Margaret sat back but then jumped forward again. "This may sound a little funny," she began, "but can you see anyone following us?"

The driver looked into the mirror and studied the old woman in the back seat. "You think someone's following you?"

"Yes. I'm not crazy. Please take a look."

The cabbie's eyes narrowed and swept the block behind them. "Well, lady, two cars and one van made the turn. When we make the next turn we'll see what happens." Margaret sank back down in the seat. "If someone is following, I can try to lose them," he continued, "but in this Saturday traffic it won't be easy."

"That won't be necessary," she said. "I just thought of where I want you to drop me."

The cab swung south on Central Park West and started downtown. The cabbie kept his eyes on the street behind him. "I think it's the van," he said. "The other two cars turned off. You in any kind of trouble?"

"Plenty," she went on. "How far back is he?"

"About a block, maybe less. Want me to drop you at the police station?"

She paused. "No, just keep going. Drop me off in front of the Museum of Natural History."

"The museum?" The driver turned around in his seat. "You sure you know what you're doing, lady?"

"You know of a better place to lose somebody?"

He shrugged. "Suit yourself."

"Do me a favor," she added. "See if you can pick up another block on him."

The driver nodded. "Here goes," he said, stepping down on the gas.

"Hey, they're gaining on us," Mund observed. "Step on it."

The van spurted ahead, but the cab was still pulling away from them.

"Shit, doesn't this thing go any faster?" Mund yelled. "They're almost two blocks ahead of us. I said step on it!" He brought the pistol up again and pointed it at the young man's chest.

"That's all it'll do, man. Can't you feel the shimmy? It's ten years old. We go any faster and we'll end up in someone's lobby." He knew Mund wouldn't shoot. The van was going too fast.

"Watch out!" the driver said, slamming his foot on the brake. The light changed and they narrowly missed a car pulling out across the street.

"You could've made it if you'd gone a little faster."

"I told you it wouldn't do it, man. There would've been three dead bodies." He shifted into first gear and started out again through the red light. If he was going to be shot it would happen now. He looked straight ahead and sped up, but the cab was nowhere in sight. The driver smiled to himself. Of course he could have made it.

Now, if something else would only delay them.

"There it is," Mund yelled. "Next to the museum." The driver saw the cab pulling out from the curb two blocks away. He couldn't see into the back seat but glanced up at the entrance in time to see an old woman struggling up the stairs. He eased up on the gas.

"Stop in front," Mund said.

Traffic was light. There was nothing else the driver could do to stall.

As the van stopped at the curb, Mund jumped out and started running up the stairs. He knew she couldn't have gone far.

Margaret was familiar with the museum from all of the Sunday afternoons she had spent there, and she headed straight for the Hall of African Mammals, the largest and darkest room she knew, a room with a lot of big picture-windows showing animals in their natural habitats. She was grateful for the crowds that were circulating around the room, and she quickly plunged into the midst of the largest group. About twenty-five people were clustered around a display showing two antelopes. She forced herself in toward the front, making sure she was surrounded by other people, but she still didn't feel safe. She would have to wait through three more exhibits before her group reached the exit.

When her group shifted to the next display, thinning out in the movement, Margaret had to rush to keep hidden. She turned as the crowd shifted slightly and caught sight of the rest of the room and quickly turned back. He was there, carefully checking each group before moving on. He was still near the entrance, but it wouldn't take him long to get to her. When she looked again he had moved up. Only four displays stood between them.

She eyed the exit nervously. One more display and she could slip out. He was only three exhibits away now and at this pace he'd find her while they were still at the last window. She had to get them moving. She edged herself out of the group and took a step toward the next exhibit. Once at the perimeter, she spoke excitedly, though in a low voice so only those close by could hear.

"Well, will you look at this! Why, I don't believe I've ever seen anything like it," she said, pretending to step up to the next window. Heads turned, and slowly part of her group broke away and sauntered past her, gradually pulling the others with them. Soon the group swelled to within five feet of the exit. She hesitated, waiting for them to go on to the next room, but no one made a move. There was nothing else she could do. Her hand tightened on the top of the fish bag. The man was only one window away, and it would take him just a minute or less to get at her. She cowered at the end of the line, but finally a few people left for the next hall, enough to cover Margaret's escape, and she turned through the doorway and ran in front of them, passing the door to the Department of Herpetology but stopping short when she realized that the ladies' room was right next to it.

She sighed with relief when she found the bathroom empty, and she chose a stall next to the wall, locked the door, and sat down to wait. It was 1:15. She would give herself two hours.

Forty minutes passed. Each time the door opened she tensed up, expecting to see a man's shoe appear in front of her stall. If he was going to check the ladies' room he would have done so by now, she thought hopefully. But at the thought of exposing herself again, she sank back in her hard seat, resolved to wait until there was no question that he had given up.

Mund didn't see Margaret leave the African Mammal Hall. He finished checking the remaining people and then went on to the Birds of the Pacific Room. He knew he couldn't check the entire museum or even keep an eye on all the exits, and he soon returned to the main entrance hall to think about his plan. He only hoped she was still around, hiding in some small corner, afraid to come out.

An idea came to him as a group of small boys entered the building. He took out his wallet and counted the several bills inside as he watched the boys deciding where to go. The tallest boy seemed to be the leader. Mund approached him and held out six five dollar bills.

"Hey, mister, watcha want?" the boy asked. He stared at the money while the other five crowded around and waited to see what would happen.

"Listen," Mund began. "I want you kids to help me. An old lady just stole my watch. Right here in the museum." He showed them an empty wrist.

"Yeah, so what?" the tall boy said.

"There's thirty dollars here," Mund said. "Five for each of you. All you have to do is watch the exits. If she leaves, I want you to tell me." The boys left him for a moment and started to huddle, but Mund sidled up to them again. "Oh, yeah, one more thing. Whoever spots her first gets another five."

"What's she look like?" one of the younger boys asked.

It had seemed to do the trick.

"Oh, 'bout seventy, carrying a red umbrella and a brown paper bag. Blue dress, white hair, pudgy." Mund held his hand up to indicate how tall she was. "This high."

"Want us to follow her around?" the taller boy said.

"No. I want one of you at each exit. Soon as you see her, come and get me. I'll be waiting by the information desk." The leader grabbed the money and handed one bill to each of the boys while Mund checked the floor map. He led them through the museum, dropping off one boy at each of the four side exits and leaving two to cover the large main entrance.

"Brilliant," he congratulated himself. He had the whole museum under surveillance. If she was inside, she was trapped. He figured that the farthest exit was only a minute round trip from where he stood. She couldn't get too far in a minute. A block, maybe two. He smugly looked up at the clock above his head, pleased with his resourcefulness. 1:45. Anytime now, he thought, keeping an eye open for the return of one of his watchdogs.

The groceries were starting to feel heavy on Margaret's lap and the bottom of the bag was getting damp. She looked at her watch for the tenth time. Only an hour and a half had gone by. Enough, she thought. She was stiff from sitting in one position for so long and her left foot was asleep.

She walked with a slight limp as she snuck out of the stall, emerging slowly, her umbrella first, ready to defend herself.

A young girl who was washing her hands looked into the mirror above her head and smiled politely as Margaret hobbled toward her. She watched Margaret put her grocery bag down on the edge of the sink, but was startled when Margaret caught her glance and turned to speak to her.

"Listen, dear, I'm in a bit of a mess. There's a man somewhere out there who wants to hurt me. He's been following me all afternoon. If he sees me leaving here I'll be in a lot of trouble," Margaret continued. "I was wondering if you could help?"

"What could I do?" the girl asked, looking nervously toward the door.

"Please. Just go and see if there is a man waiting outside the door. If there is, come back and tell me. It's really not very much trouble, dear."

The girl adjusted the strap of her pocketbook. "What

does he look like?" she asked, as her hand reached for the door.

Margaret gave her as detailed a description as she could and whispered her thanks as the girl left. Margaret paced back and forth, but, after five minutes, she picked up her bag, grabbed her umbrella, and pushed cautiously through the door. She remembered that one of the museum's exits led directly into the subway from the lowest level, near the cafeteria. There were sure to be hundreds of people milling around and it would certainly be the safest way to leave the museum.

She found a staircase and eased herself down the flights to the basement level. She stopped behind a pillar to calm herself and inspect the faces. The constant movement of the crowd made a good survey difficult, but she soon felt safe and quickly walked through the middle of the crowd. She didn't see the man and no one gave her a second glance except a sweet little boy at the exit who smiled at her.

She hurried through the doors to the uptown subway. It was one of the longest stations on the line, its platform running more than two blocks. The train always stopped somewhere in the middle and Margaret placed herself so she could get into the first car. There were about ten other people on the platform, a small crowd, but at least she wasn't alone. She relaxed a little when she heard a faint rumbling. She walked to the edge and leaned over to look down the tunnel, feeling reassured as the headlights came toward her.

"Thank heaven," she breathed, stepping back to wait for the train.

Mund was getting impatient. An hour had passed and none of the boys had reported in. He leaned against the information booth, swearing to himself. Thirty bucks thrown away. He clenched his fist and looked toward the main entrance. The two kids were still there, eying each person who left.

"Hey, mister, I get the other five dollars." It was just a

noise coming from the jumble of sounds in the lobby. Mund didn't react at first, but then he wheeled around and saw the kid pushing past a group of people and heading toward him. It was one of the smaller boys, the one who was downstairs by the subway. "I saw her, I saw her," he kept repeating as he held out his hand.

"Where?"

"Into the subway. She went into the subway." The boy nearly screamed his delight as he looked to the main entrance to see if his friends had noticed he'd won. When he turned around again, his empty hand outstretched, Mund was already twenty yards away, running toward the stairs. The boy considered chasing, but it was no good, the man was running too fast for him. He grabbed nervously in his pants pocket for the original five dollars and turned dejectedly to find his friends.

Margaret started to board the train, but froze in midstep. A man had pushed through the crowd at the exit and was running toward her. She watched, transfixed, as he raced for the train.

The doors clicked and Margaret just managed to squeeze inside before they slid shut behind her. Trembling, she fell back against the doors as the train jolted to a start. He had been fifteen yards away from the last car.

Mund kept running as the train pulled out. He had seen her and was determined to keep running even if he had to run along the tracks to the next station. For several seconds the train maintained a slow pace as the cars jerked against one another. Mund closed the gap to ten feet and then five. The train started to pick up speed, but for one last instant he was running faster and threw himself toward the back of the train. If he had fallen he would have broken his neck, but somehow one of his hands grasped a metal bar and the other wrist caught in the top V groove of the steel safety gate. His body crashed against the back platform and he heard his gun clatter onto the tracks.

The wind was partially knocked out of him, but he

managed to cling to the gate. He watched the tracks speed by under his dangling feet, struggling to catch his breath, and then slowly pulled himself onto the narrow platform. The train surged through the tunnel throwing him from side to side. He was breathing hard and felt his lungs constrict at the intake of dirty air. He felt like vomiting. Over his shoulder he could still see the Eighty-first Street station receding behind him, the platform lights fading until there was one small dot, and then blackness as the train rounded a curve. He tried the back door, but it was locked. There were several people inside but no one saw him.

When the train finally pulled into the Eighty-sixth Street station, he jumped over the back gate and onto the platform. He started running up alongside the train, trying to get closer to the front car, but he made it only a third of the way before the doors started to close. He pushed inside the crowded car and managed to hold the door open while he watched the people exit through the turnstiles.

She was not one of them.

He looked up the platform to see if she might be hiding behind a pillar and only let go when he was satisfied she was still on the train. As it started up again, he looked down at his hands, still red and scratched from his leap. No, he thought. It didn't matter at all that he had lost his gun.

Margaret had nervously peered out the door when the train stopped. She had seen him run up the platform but before she knew it the doors had closed, trapping her inside. She sat down, waiting, too startled to think of any alternative. The few other people in the car looked too self-involved and she knew it was hopeless to approach them.

Margaret swayed with the motion of the train and braced herself to the seat with her hands. Her umbrella fell to the floor and she looked down at it dully, and then slowly, thoughtfully, picked it up. It was the only weapon she had and it just might work.

When she reached the end of the car she saw him coming toward her. Quickly opening the door, she stepped out

across the platform and fitted the square top of her umbrella behind the sliding handle of the opposite door. She
tried to angle the tip toward the doorjamb but it was an
inch too short. He was still coming, still grinning. She
looked around frantically. The bag! She quickly emptied
the fish onto the floor and began folding the heavy brown
paper bag. It would only take three folds, but it wasn't
wide enough. One more would do it. She tried again, forc-
ing what little strength she had to complete the fold. It was
a strain and she brought the wad close to her body for more
leverage. The paper started to bend slowly, enough to give
her the wedge she needed. She repositioned the umbrella
and forced the paper into the gap, hammering it into position with her fist.

She fell back heavily against the car, almost faint from
the effort. Mund was only two feet away and reaching for
the handle. He pushed down lightly and gave a slight tug,
but the handle wouldn't move.

He tried again with two hands. Margaret held her breath
as the umbrella bent slightly. For a moment, it looked as if
it might break but it snapped rigidly back into place. She
watched him through the glass as he continued to struggle.

The train was slowing. In another minute they would be
in the station and all the doors would open.

Margaret unhinged the side gate and pushed it to one
side. The only thing between her and the wall rushing by
was a set of steel fenders. There was a space between
them, perhaps six inches, when the cars were in line but
the gap closed entirely around some of the sharper turns.

The fenders were near the outer edge of the train, past
the end of the platform, about four feet away from where
Margaret stood. The only way to get there was to climb out
on the supporting I beams. Margaret looked down at the
polished steel track slipping by, and then again at the gap
between the fenders. If she tried to pass through when the
train was in a curve she would never make it.

As the train braked she took a last look at Mund. He
was watching her every move.

She passed into the first car. The lights of the Ninety-sixth Street station were just starting to appear in the front window, but they were several yards away. Her timing would have to be perfect. She held on to one of the poles and waited until the lights of the station were fifteen feet away, then reached up and pulled the emergency brake.

She was tossed violently forward, but managed to keep from falling. The train screeched and lurched, throwing the passengers from side to side until it stopped.

Margaret rushed out to the platform between the two cars. The station was just beyond the opening between the fenders, and without looking down she edged herself up onto the beam and cautiously eased herself outward. If the train started up again she'd be thrown onto the track. She fixed on the opening and inched herself along the beams until she reached it. Her left leg pushed through and she gained a footing on the platform. She struggled and squirmed, finally managing to get the middle of her body between the two fenders. She paused for breath, pressed between the two pieces of steel, and she sensed the weight of the train pressing against her. A little jerk and she would be crushed. She shuddered at the thought of it and continued to free herself as quickly as she could. In a few seconds she was on the platform and running through the exit doors.

Mund picked himself off the floor. He had been slammed into the glass, and blood spurted from his nose. He could just see Margaret rushing down the platform and toward the exit, and he ran to the end of his car only to see the platform stop and the dark, close wall of the tunnel begin. There was no way for him to get out between the cars.

In two minutes the engine started up again. Mund waited by the doors, but the train idled for several minutes before it started to crawl into the station. When the doors opened, Mund was the first out, and he raced furiously for the stairs.

Margaret sighed with relief when she emerged from the exit. Her sewing and knitting group met only two blocks away, and she knew she could count on them for shelter.

She was totally exhausted and shaking uncontrollably, and she had to move slowly, pausing against parked cars every few steps to catch her breath and steady herself.

When she reached the building, she climbed the stairs to the door and collapsed against the buzzer.

"Hurry up," she gasped, keeping her finger on the bell. "Come on." She looked behind her and searched the length of the street to the subway exit. She hadn't been fast enough.

He was running across Amsterdam and looking right at her. She leaned against the door, hoping to blend with it, but it opened suddenly and she lost her balance and fell to the floor inside.

"Margaret..."

It was a friend of hers, one of the women from her group.

"Quick," she cried, "lock the door and follow me." She struggled to her feet and led the woman to the back of the building, behind the staircase. "We have only a minute," she gasped as the woman started to interrupt.

"For God's sake, listen!" Margaret yelled.

Mund paused briefly at the front door to read a plaque on the wall. "United Order of True Sisters," he said aloud as he found the buzzer and pushed the button in. Two minutes later, the door was slowly opened by an old woman in a faded dress.

"Yes?" she asked.

"A woman just came in here," Mund said, sticking his foot inside the door. "I've got to see her."

"I think you're mistaken," she answered. "No one's come in, not for at least an hour. Perhaps you've confused this with next door." She nodded to her left. "The houses look much the same and many people make that mistake." She tried to close the door but Mund forced his way into the vestibule.

"Look, goddamn it. I don't make mistakes. If you don't want to get hurt, quit stalling." He grabbed the woman's arm and turned her around. "Take me to her."

"Please don't hurt me," she cried. "Please. She asked me to do it."

"Where is she?"

"In the workroom."

He gave her a push forward. "Show me."

The woman reluctantly led Mund up the dark staircase. The building smelled musty and the stairs creaked under their feet. The second-floor hallway was ill lit, but he could see down the end of it to a large heavy door with bright light coming out from under a crack.

"You first," he whispered, prodding the woman with his fist. "And don't try to warn her."

The woman nodded, opened the door, and took a step into the room. Mund followed and stood next to her. It was a fairly large room, filled with sewing machines, looms, and tables with balls of yarn piled on top of them. About twenty old women sat scattered around the room. Most of them were knitting, but they stopped when they saw Mund walk in.

They're scared, he thought to himself. His eyes searched their faces. Margaret's was not one of them.

"Okay, where is she?"

He heard the door slam behind him and turned to see the woman he had followed lock it from the inside. He saw her move toward the open window and he tried to stop her, but just as he reached her, the woman threw the key out of the window. It landed on the sill, bounced once, then fell out of view.

The woman slowly turned around to face him. "If it's Mrs. Binton you're looking for, she left a moment ago." She smiled innocently.

Mund ran to the door and jerked the handle up and down, trying to force it.

"It's no good," she said. "That door's withstood the ravages of over one hundred years' abuse. I think you'll find it quite solid."

He kicked at the door but it didn't budge. It didn't even vibrate.

"The janitor will be here at five-thirty," she continued. "He has the other key. May I suggest that you sit down and make yourself useful? The ladies are always looking for someone to size their sweaters on."

Mund stormed toward her.

"No, really, young man, do sit down." She nodded over her shoulder to the other women in the room.

He stopped and turned to look around him. Each woman held a long, gleaming knitting needle. They were all pointed at him.

# Twenty

"WHAT TOOK YOU SO LONG?" SID asked anxiously as Margaret entered the apartment. "Bertie and I were so worried. She really gave me hell when I came back without you, but I can't blame her, or any of us, for that matter. We never should have let you go. She left a few minutes ago to ask everyone else if they'd seen you."

"I'll tell you all about it," she said heavily, "but first, give me a drink."

Sid found a half bottle of scotch in Bertie's kitchen and poured a small glass for Margaret and a large one for himself.

"You still have the flyers?" she asked, after she had taken a sip of her drink.

"Yes," he said, pointing to the dining table. "But the bagels got lost in all the confusion."

"No matter." She smiled. "The fish didn't make it either. Well, I certainly got my exercise. If you promise not to get upset, I'll tell you what happened." She sat back, propped up her feet, and described her adventure, and when she had finished Sid told her what had happened in Rebach's.

"They must be getting desperate," Margaret concluded. "I'm sorry to have caused you so much trouble."

Sid looked over at Margaret and smiled. He raised his

glass to her and poured the rest of his drink down his throat.

"You know, Sid," Margaret said, raising her glass and doing the same. "I've never felt so popular in my life. Or is it unpopular? I can't figure out which."

Early the next morning, everyone assembled at Bertie's. They discussed what had happened to Margaret and Sid, and everyone listened carefully as Margaret went over the plan. They were determined not to let anything go wrong this time.

Pancher left at 9:00 to deliver the flyers, and at 9:15 the others left and took up their positions on the benches across the street from the building.

Sid, who had devised an elaborate system of signals, crossed the street and disappeared into the building while the others watched. Only Rena and Durso remained behind with Margaret.

Five minutes later, Sid came out smiling. He winked, pulled at his cap and sauntered across the street. He positioned himself so he would have a good view. Two minutes later Pancher emerged and left for Bertie's, giving his hat a tug before he reached the corner. Everything was set. The doorman came out shortly and stood with his hands behind his back as he casually inspected every tenant who left.

Daker reached across his desk and picked up his mail. Most of it looked like bills. He glanced briefly at the A & P circular, and started to toss it out, but stopped in mid-motion. He carefully reread the piece of paper. "Special. Cane Sugar and Plastic Garbage Bags. An Offer You Can't Refuse." Daker crumpled the paper, threw it on the floor, and slammed his hand down on the buzzer.

"Cotlin, get your ass in here," he yelled. When Cotlin burst into the room he pointed to the crumpled paper. "Find out where this came from."

Cotlin bent over to pick up the paper and slowly smoothed it out on the top of Daker's desk. "Jesus . . ."

Daker nodded. "Check it out right away. Ask some of

the others on the floor if they got one, then check it out with the store. The coincidence is just a little unbelievable. There aren't even any prices on it." He thought for a moment. "You still got that sugar Mund lifted from Longley's place?"

Cotlin stiffened. "Yeah, I put it away."

"Well, then, I can't figure it out. Got to be a coincidence, that's all. But check it anyway."

Cotlin left Daker's office wondering whether it was even possible that someone could have found the sugar in the garbage. It just didn't seem likely.

He ran down the back stairs to the basement and searched for the superintendent. When Cotlin finally found him, his suspicions were confirmed. A garbage can had been missing for a day. The super had thought it odd but hadn't checked into it since it had reappeared the day after.

Cotlin thanked him and went upstairs to the lobby. Maybe he was being too nervous. Maybe it was nothing at all.

"Morning, Mr Cotlin." The doorman smiled at him.

"Morning," Cotlin said, as he walked out of the building.

The doorman faced the benches across the street and tipped his hat twice.

Sid watched the doorman signal. 4B, he said to himself . . . Daker. He motioned to Rose, who got up from her bench and headed for the corner.

She had a hard time keeping up with Cotlin. He had long swift strides and though she was trying to look as inconspicuous as possible, she found herself trotting much of the way. Her bags kept bumping into her legs and throwing her off balance, and more than once she had to grab onto a mailbox or a lamppost to keep from falling.

She closed the space between them and then slowed down to catch her breath. At that moment Cotlin turned around and looked behind him, but all he saw was an old scavenger heading toward a group of garbage cans.

He crossed the avenue and quickened his pace, and as

he approached the A & P he pulled the flyer out of his coat pocket and tried to find its duplicate in the A & P windows. He didn't see any and he pushed through the door and spotted the manager talking to one of the clerks. He thrust the flyer under the manager's nose.

"This for real?"

The manager was startled and took a step away to look up at Cotlin.

"Is this legitimate?" Cotlin repeated, shoving the flyer up to the man's face. "You sent them out?"

The manager looked at it for a second and handed it back.

"Where'd you get that? It's not from A & P. Someone's playing a joke on you, mister."

Cotlin looked vacantly at the paper in his hand and then whirled around to leave. Rose was just pulling away from the window, her bags in tow, and when he ran to the entrance to look outside, she was already twenty yards away and moving uptown at a half run.

He recognized the scavenger who had been behind him a few blocks before. Funny, he thought. They usually move slowly, usually stop at every can to scrounge around.

Margaret Binton, he cursed. Mund had been unable to get her. She must be behind all this.

Cotlin started to follow Rose, walking fast and staying low. And if he guessed right, Binton's was where the old scavenger was headed. He felt the bulk of his 9-mm Beretta. He'd finish off the job that Mund had blown. Daker would be pleased. All he had to do was pick his time.

Rose reached Ninety-third Street and turned down the long block to Broadway. She was almost at Bertie's. What luck to have gotten the proof we needed, she thought. Margaret'll be real proud of me. She was waiting on the corner for the light to change when she felt the hand on her arm.

"Rose Gaffery?"

"Yes," she said, startled.

"Please come with me," Jacobson said. "Lieutenant Morley would like to speak to you."

# Twenty-one

"SO YOU HAVEN'T SEEN HER FOR A couple of weeks?" Morley's brow wrinkled as he looked at his notes.

"No, the last time was when she was feeding the pigeons. Already told you a million times." Rose was scared, but the one thing she knew she couldn't do was to give away Margaret's hiding place.

"Rose," Morley said sighing. "I told you what the problem is. Your friend is in serious danger and we have to find her. We need your help."

"I'm trying to help," Rose said.

"Please try to remember. Anything, a name, an address, anything at all she might have mentioned." Morley waited.

"Nope. Don't know nothin' else." Rose sat back for several moments and stared at the corner of the desk.

Jacobson looked at his watch. "It's no good, Lieutenant, we've been here all afternoon."

Morley took a long drag from his cigarette and slowly blew out the smoke. "I hope you're telling the truth, Rose. Because if you're not, and Margaret gets hurt, it will be your fault. Have you anything more to say?"

Rose shook her head and fumbled nervously with her bags.

"Okay, you can go." Morley shook his head as the door

closed. "I don't think she'd lie," he said. "Not when her friend's life is at stake. Go back to Broadway and keep watch. If you see Schaeffer, tell him to stop looking for Gaffery."

"Thank God," Rose mumbled as she walked out of the building. When she reached Ninetieth Street, she slid onto an empty bench in Riverside Park. She needed to rest for a while and to plan her strategy. She shouldn't go to Bertie's right away—a policeman might have followed her.

Cotlin had followed Rose to the precinct and had waited outside, puzzled by her reaction to the cop. If she were a part of Binton's scheme she wouldn't have looked so scared, but he thought he'd better follow her anyway, to be doubly safe.

Rose left the park after two hours and Cotlin followed. When she stopped abruptly, he ducked behind a car and watched her search the street and then rush into a building. By the time he had crossed the street and entered the lobby the elevator was on its way up. He watched until the indicator stopped at five and then found the door to the back stairs.

The fifth floor hallway was filled with the sound of many excited voices. Cotlin followed them to the end of the hall and paused outside a door. When he heard Rose and Margaret talking he reached for his Beretta, but paused in mid-motion. Too many people in there, he thought. And one was all he needed.

He went back to the stairwell and stood behind the door. The frosted glass window gave him enough of a view to see shapes pass by.

"The cops stopped me," Rose continued, her voice slow and serious. "They're looking for you, just like you said. Didn't tell them nothin'."

Roosa looked skeptical. "Maybe they followed you here," he said.

Rose shook her head. "Waited for a long time in the park to make sure. A long time. Weren't no one around. 'S okay. Margaret's safe."

"Yes, thank God," Margaret said. "Only Mr. Daker checked on his flyer—he's the one we want."

"You did it!" Rena broke out, clapping her hands together. "You did it."

"Thank you all," Margaret said as everyone broke out into applause. "Now, how about a celebration drink. I brought a bottle of sherry and I think it's time I opened it. Bertie, let's get some glasses for a toast. I'll turn on the lamp—it's getting dark in here."

"A toast to us," she offered. Ten glasses tipped amid the cheers and laughter and the sherry bottle was soon empty.

Cotlin watched as the guests started filtering out. Seven had left so far, but the room was still filled with conversation. When the time came, it would be fast. In, and out.

Bertie and Rena sat on the couch finishing the sherry some of the others had left in their glasses.

"Shame to throw it out," Rena said as she gathered the rest of the glasses around her.

Margaret was impatient to finish her plan and excused herself to Bertie and Rena. She pulled out a pen and some paper and sat down at the table on the other side of the couch.

She wanted to write it all down, from start to finish: the story of the search, the grocery flyers, the names of her friends, the results of it all. She didn't want there to be any doubt in anyone's mind about the sequence of events and the important facts they had uncovered. After the first few sentences she got up to get the lamp. It was the only light that was on in the room, and she set it down on her table next to the empty sherry bottle.

"Hey," Rena said. "I can see you want me to leave." She got up but tottered briefly and sat back down on the couch. "A little dizzy I guess. I'm not used to so much sherry."

Bertie helped her to her feet and steadied her. "I'll help her home," she whispered to Margaret. "Rena," she said, turning to take her friend's arm, "it's not too far, is it?"

"No, I can make it."

"Come on," Bertie said. "I'll go with you. I could use some fresh air." She steadied Rena and steered her toward the door. "Don't bother locking it," she called to Margaret. "I'll be back soon."

"Take your time," Margaret said.

The door closed and Margaret finished her first page. She was tired, but wanted to complete her work before she went to bed. First things first though, Margaret thought, glad for the silence as she went over to the phone and dialed a number.

"Sergeant Schaeffer, please," she said quietly, trying not to sound excited.

"I'm sorry. He's left for the day. Do you want me to give him a message?"

"Is Lieutenant Morley there?"

"No, he left also."

Margaret hesitated. "Yes, tell Sergeant Schaeffer that Mrs. Binton called. Yes, Binton, B-I-N-T-O-N. I have some information for him. He can reach me at TR6-5834."

She hung up, a bit disappointed, and went back to her writing. When she got to the part where they had dragged the can home, she felt a slight draft on her neck. She looked up from her work and her eyes focused on Cotlin's face, leering out from the dim light at the far side of the room. Her hand froze on her pen. She tried to scream, but no sound came out.

Cotlin leveled his Beretta at Margaret's chest.

"Remember me?"

Margaret nodded slowly. "Yes, I remember. You offered me a trip to Florida, didn't you?"

He grinned. "I'll never understand you old ladies. Always meddling around, always screwing things up." His finger tightened around the trigger as the phone rang.

"Don't get it," he ordered. He could have pulled the trigger right then, but for some reason he wanted to wait for the phone to stop. In some peculiar way, he felt as though someone were listening.

It's Schaeffer, thought Margaret, grasping for a small spark of hope. The Beretta was no more than two feet away. If I can only stall him, she thought, maybe Schaeffer will come over.

The rings stopped and Cotlin took a step forward.

"Don't you want to see what I'm writing?" she asked. "I think it might interest you."

For the first time since he had entered the room Cotlin took his eyes off Margaret and looked at the neat handwriting that covered the page.

"What is it?"

"It's the story of how I found out who you were. The whole thing." She managed a smile. "Would make interesting reading for the police, don't you think?"

Cotlin reached over and grabbed the paper. He held it up and quickly read the first sentence, then crumpled it and stuffed it into his pocket.

"Pity they'll never read it," he said.

"Oh, but they will," she sighed. "Unless you find the other copies I wrote."

"What other copies?"

"Well, you see I'm not so good at writing. I find it hard to keep all my thoughts collected and in order." She pointed at his pocket. "What you have there is a result of several awkward starts, each one with different amounts of information." She leaned back. Would he go for it? she wondered. "If you want to be thorough, I think you'd better get all of them."

He looked at her for a few seconds, searching for any sign that she was lying. She returned his gaze without flinching.

"Where are they?"

"I threw them out."

"Where?"

She gave him her brightest smile. "Don't expect me to do your work for you."

Cotlin hesitated. Out of the corner of his eye he could see the kitchen and the small garbage can a few steps away. It wouldn't take long to check her story.

"How many others were there?" he asked.

Margaret shook her head and smiled.

Cotlin carted the garbage can to the center of the living room and dumped it on the floor. Still holding the gun on her, he began to look through the garbage.

"How does it feel?" she asked. "Is it fun?"

Cotlin said nothing, and in about two minutes, he had finished looking and stood up.

"There's the bedroom, too," she offered, pointing to the closed door.

"Get it," he said, motioning with the gun.

"Of course." She stood up and walked into the bedroom and picked up the basket.

"Over here," he said. "Now sit down."

She moved back to her seat behind the table. This isn't taking long enough, she thought. There must be something else. As she sat down again, her right foot brushed against the cord of the table lamp.

Cotlin kicked over the wastebasket and sent the contents spilling onto the floor. As he was going through its contents, Margaret wound the lamp cord around her foot.

"Aren't you forgetting something?" she asked. "All those nice fingerprints?"

"Let me worry about that," he snarled, raising the gun, but before he had even aimed, Margaret pulled out the light plug with her foot and screamed, dropping to the floor as Cotlin pulled the trigger. The sound of the shot was almost deafening in the small room, but he heard her cry out and knew he had hit her. The room was pitch black and he stood motionless, waiting for some sound to indicate where she was. He heard her crawling, but his eyes hadn't yet adjusted to the darkness and he couldn't tell where she was.

Margaret rested on her knees and elbows under the table. The shot had grazed her left arm and she could feel the warm blood flowing down to her elbow. She felt along the floor and found the lamp cord, and although she couldn't see into the room, the crack under the front door provided enough light for her to tell where Cotlin's feet were. She quietly looped the electric wire into a large circle and laid it out on the floor in front of her feet. Then she reached up into her hair and withdrew the four-inch steel hatpin she always wore.

Cotlin stepped closer and tried to peer into the darkness. His eyes were slowly adjusting and he paused a minute to focus ont the figure that was taking shape under the table.

Margaret saw his foot step into the circle of cord, and she tugged it closed with one hand while she thrust the hatpin deep into his calf with the other.

Cotlin screamed and fired a shot, but it bore through the wood table, missing Margaret's neck by inches. Margaret held on to the cord as she heard Cotlin topple over backward onto the floor. He grabbed at his calf and dropped the gun, sending it clattering across the wood floor.

Margaret scrambled to her feet and started throwing things in his direction. Anything she could grab: glasses, the pen, the lamp. She finally grabbed the sherry bottle and threw it. Everything crashed when it landed, everything except the sherry bottle, which landed with a dull thud. She heard a long groan, and then nothing. Her arm hurt slightly, but she waited by the table until she was sure Cotlin was out cold. She managed to get herself to the kitchen and leaned against the doorjamb, still shaking. When she had calmed down a bit, she felt around in a drawer for a knife, and then ventured back into the living room and turned on a light.

Margaret slowly went over to where Cotlin was lying. She wasn't sure how long he would remain unconscious. The lamp was in pieces around him, as were the shattered remains of everything else she had thrown. The cord was still wound round his feet. Margaret tied it into a solid knot and then cut the strings off Bertie's apron and wound them around his wrists. It took a long time to roll him over to the sofa, and when she got him there, she tied his feet to one end and his wrists to the other and sat down to rest.

When she heard the door open, she jumped up, startled, and raised her knife.

"Easy, Margaret, easy," Schaeffer said. "I got your message. You okay?"

Margaret smiled. "Better than he is," she said, pointing

behind the couch. "It's my friend from Squire's. I called to tell you about him, but now you can meet him in person." A low groan sounded from behind the couch. "He had offered me Florida, but I think that right now I'll just go home. I'm not ready to retire. Not just yet."

# About the Author

Richard Barth is a goldsmith and an instructor at the Fashion Institute of Technology. He lives in Manhattan with his wife and two children. THE RAG BAG CLAN is the first book in the Margaret Binton mystery series.

# White-haired grandmother...

# &

## free-lance CIA agent...

# DOROTHY GILMAN'S
## Mrs. Pollifax Novels